The 18th Pale Descendant

William Muir
The 18th Pale Descendant

Quartet Books

First published by Quartet Books in 2001
A member of the Namara Group
27 Goodge Street
London W1P 2LD

A catalogue entry for this book is available from the British Library

ISBN 0 7043 8161 3

Phototypeset by FiSH Books, London
Printed and bound in Finland by WS Bookwell

For Kathryn

Contents

The Letter

Fate had been conspiring against William Riley Scott for days. Every second, while he was working, fucking, watching TV, fate had never let up. And only now, on this bright October Monday morning, was it prepared to make itself known.

At 7.49 a.m. he still had all that was familiar. As usual he was already awake and lay in complete contentment. Body relaxed to the point that for him it no longer existed. He watched the second hand on the clock as it journeyed round the numbers. This was precious time, before the day really began. During this time no one could intrude on him. At 7.49 and fifty seconds he reached over and switched off the alarm before the buzzing tone could escape and destroy his peace at 7.50.

He rose and went through to the living room. Outside, three storeys below, the world was already getting under way. Bus queues were forming and traffic ploughed the streets. He turned on the television.

'And so today I'm afraid it's raincoats and umbrellas as we see persistent showers throughout the country and temperatures failing to rise into double figures.' The young girl on screen pointed to a picture of a cloud so Riley should know how to recognize it should he see one. For at this moment, and this made him smile, the sky was a perfect blue.

The telephone rang. He knew who was calling before he answered. Only one person phoned at this time of day.

'Hello, Clara.'

'Sorry, I know it's early, but I've got a million and one things to do today and I wouldn't have got a chance later.'

Clara always called early and always had a million and one things to do.

'It's no problem.'

'I just wanted to check that everything was still OK for tonight.'

'Sure. Why shouldn't it be?'

'No reason.'

'You don't wish to make alternative arrangements do you Clara?'

'No. Of course not.' A slight pause and her voice became coy. 'Tell me, has big boy seen little boy today?'

'No, I don't believe he has.'

'Good. I'd like it to stay that way.'

'Why?'

'Because I'd like to pay a visit to little boy myself.'

'I'm sure that can be arranged.'

Riley put the receiver down.

On his way to the shower the mail dropped on to the doormat. Four letters. Nothing unusual. Letters arrived every day. But this was fate with the first intrusion into the life of William Riley Scott.

Morning in the bathroom was a ritual. He stopped at the mirror above the washbasin to study his face. In his teen years he had suffered badly from acne and the taunts of his friends. Now his skin was slightly scarred and not unknown, though he was thirty-one years old, to break out in spots. Today, much to his relief, it was clear. His fingertips probed his chin and ran down the slopes of his throat. He felt bristles but decided they weren't long enough to warrant the much-detested shave.

He switched on the shower, stripped off his shorts and stood under the cascading hot water. It hit him square in the chest. Burning his skin. Reaching deep into his bones. He worked up a lather with the soap and covered himself in its creamy texture. His eyes closed. He saw the redhead who had sat opposite him on the bus the evening before. The top of her head would barely clear his shoulders. And plump. Her hair in a bob. She had big eyes and a large mouth. Her fingers covered in cheap gold rings. As she left the bus he had been hypnotized by her large behind tightly encased in jeans. She had glanced at him once.

He liked to imagine how it would start. She would leave something 'accidentally' on the seat as she got up. Her bag. No. Her purse. Being a gentleman, he would of course pursue her in an attempt to return the forgotten item. Grateful, she would invite him to her house for coffee. Or perhaps they were already there and he had to explain why he was knocking on her door. She was laughing. Her mouth open and wide. Red-coated lips. Saying she hadn't even missed her purse. Asking him to come in. As she filled the kettle at the kitchen sink, he came up behind her. Cupping her breasts. She squirmed against him. Letting loose a deep sigh. He unbuttoned her blouse. She moaned and pulled the bra away herself. Forcing his mouth on to her nipple. His tongue tasted metal and he bit down on the flesh and the ring that pierced it. His hand jerked rhythmically on his cock, but it wasn't his hand it was hers. Covered in cheap gold rings. He had her bent over a kitchen worktop. His fingers fumbling with the studs on her jeans. Tugging and exposing her pale thighs. She guided him into her. His eyes opened and the white tiles of the bathroom momentarily blinded him before he saw his sperm disappear into the water and subsequently down the drain.

A shiver ran through Riley as he rinsed himself and reached for the towel. He carefully combed back his long black hair while scrutinizing the significance, if there was any, to the pierced nipple. This had become a regular detail in his dreams lately and seemed to give him an added thrill. He had never known anyone with piercings. Perhaps it was a sign of too much magazine-reading.

Since he didn't own many clothes, dressing took only a couple of minutes. Black trousers, white shirt, black socks. He settled on the settee that sometimes doubled as a bed with his letters and his coffee.

The first was an electricity bill. He didn't bother to open it since it was blue not red and therefore unworthy of his attention. He sipped his coffee, keeping one eye on the television, which was playing a report on another proposed peace plan for the Middle East, where fighting had again broken out. For a moment he was spellbound by the image of a dusty street with half a dozen people running for cover as gunshots were fired at them. He'd seen a riot once when travelling in Indonesia. He'd been on his way to the train station in Jakarta with a friend when they'd entered a street filled with thousands of people wearing red bandannas, red shirts, chanting, waving placards. The police charged and Riley ran for the station with his friend. An Indonesian man close behind them tripped on the kerb and fell. Riley stopped. He could still see the pain in the man's eyes and hear the dull thump of the blows as the policeman set on him with a long wooden pole.

The second letter was from his daughter. The A4 sheet of writing paper filled with five lines in the carefully practised and concentrated writing of a seven-year-old.

Dear Dad

How are you? I am well and missing you. I went swimming yesterday. I can almost swim by myself

with no bands. Sarah is coming over for tea so I
have to go.

Love you,
Emma

    The smile on his face widened at the sight of the flowers
drawn in blue crayon around the writing. Guilt numbed his
fingers and he almost dropped the letter returning it to its
envelope. Four weeks since he had seen her. Two weeks since
he had phoned. Familiar excuses popped into his mind. He
slipped the letter under a book on the coffee table and with it
those thoughts.

    The third letter came in a white business envelope. His
name was printed in heavy black type. Mr W. R. Scott. This
confused him, since he rarely used his first name in any
capacity. He flipped it round and studied the back. He stared
hard at the words printed in blue, then ripped the letter open.
He read it twice. Then a third time. It still didn't make any
sense.

Dear Mr Scott

I am writing to inform you that you are required
by the Department of Justice and Corrections to
report to room 712 at our Head Office, 27
Connaught Place, at 9 a.m., 20 October. Any
failure to comply to this request could result in
legal action being taken against you. Enquiries
can be made on the following number.

Riley's hand strayed to the telephone. The 20th. Today. He was supposed to be working. What did it mean by legal action? He'd run a red light three weeks ago but hadn't even received the ticket yet. Maybe it was jury service. He'd been selected. Legal action. What did it mean? He had to be at work. They should have informed him sooner. He had to work.

He realized he was sweating and laughed at his foolishness. He picked up the telephone and dialled the number. It was bound to be a mistake. The phone was answered on the second ring.

'Hello, Department of Justice and Corrections, how may I help you?'

'Can I have extension 183 please?'

'Hold the line, sir.'

The phone rang without reply. The receptionist cut back in. 'I'm afraid there's no answer on that number, sir. You could try after 9, that's when most of our offices are open.'

'But that's too late.'

'Can I be of help, sir?'

'I've just received a letter more or less ordering me to report to one of your offices at 9, but I have to work.'

'I'm afraid that if you have received a request to attend one of our offices, then I can only suggest that you do so.'

'But what's it about? Is it jury service?'

'I'm afraid I have no information as to the nature of anyone's summons to this department.'

'But I have to work and the letter mentions legal action if I don't turn up. Can you put me through to someone who can explain it?'

'One moment please.'

Fucking bitch. Her friendly, high-pitched tone was getting on his nerves.

'I'm sorry, sir, there's no one available to speak to you.'

'So what am I to do?'

'Again, I can only suggest that you comply with our request. Now, if that is all, sir, I do have other calls to deal with. Goodbye.' The line went dead.

8.30 a.m. Already too late for the bus, which meant he was going to be late for work. If only his fucking car hadn't broken down, he wouldn't need the fucking bus. And if his fucking ex-wife didn't chisel so much money out of him, then he wouldn't own a rusting shit-heap that fell apart every week. Once again his troubles in life were down to her. This train of thought made him smile.

He mulled over the conversation. Where had he gone wrong? Usually he could charm a bit on the phone. It could have been the use of the word ordered. Perhaps it was too strong, or his tone too obviously sarcastic. It probably didn't matter a shit what tone he'd used. More than likely the bitch of a receptionist had been trained to rebuff anyone who called and sound sweet in the process. He could picture her sitting back, examining her nails and laughing her arse off while he sat on hold, believing her to be scouring the building for someone to help him.

He'd have to call Andrew. Andrew would know what was going on.

'Good morning, Riley. What a pleasure it is to hear your voice.'

'You sound happy.'

'I'm sitting in five lines of stationary traffic, why shouldn't I be happy?'

'Is that the full story?'

'Not quite. I should be arriving about now at a meeting with some incredibly interesting corporate people. Unfortunately I shall have to cancel them, leaving me just enough time to drop into a little café I know and study the day's racing.'

'Well then you also have time to help me with a little problem.'

'Why not, and since I'm not due to start work now until 10 I won't even charge you.'

'How very Christian of you to spread your happiness, Andrew.'

'How very Christian of me to be kind since I know you can no longer afford me.'

'Too true.'

'So what's the problem?'

'I've just received a letter from the Department of Justice and Corrections instructing me to attend one of their offices this morning or they'll take legal action against me.'

Andrew remained silent. Riley could hear a radio and the results of pissed-off drivers pressing on their horns in the background.

'Andrew, are you still there?'

'Yes, sorry, I was thinking.'

'Don't apologize for thinking. Just tell me what you're thinking.'

'You better go.'

'But I've got to work.'

'You better go.'

'Couldn't I ring them later and explain that I only got the letter today and couldn't get off work?'

'No. If you don't show, you'll just get passed along to prosecutions and those people are speedy. Before you know it two coppers will be knocking on your boss's door to haul you away. A telephone call won't make any difference.'

'Couldn't you call?'

'It wouldn't make any difference. Have you kept the payments to your ex in order?'

'Of course.'

'Well, I know it all seems very big brother, but it's probably a mistake. Just go down and I'm sure it'll sort itself out.'

'I ran a red light a few weeks ago.'

'It's hardly a capital crime, Riley.'

'I know, I'm just worried.'

'What exactly does the letter say?'

Riley read the letter word for word. Again himself trying to decipher a meaning to it and again failing.

'What was the room number?'

'712.'

'I think it's best you go.'

Riley thought he could detect a more sombre tone to his friend's voice.

'What's wrong? Do you know something?'

'I don't know anything, Riley, but as your friend, your lawyer and fellow football player, I recommend that you go. Now, if you need me I'll be in the office this afternoon. OK?'

'Yeah.'

'It will be all right.'

'I know.'

'Bye then.'

The TV astrologer explored the ups and downs of the day's horoscopes. Today was a great day to be a Libra. Shite for Capricorns.

8.40 a.m. Fuck it, he'd go to work. What could they do? Arrest him? He hadn't done anything wrong. He put on his shoes and his jacket. Picked up his keys. Checked himself one last time in the mirror.

Maybe they would arrest him.

'Hello, Milo Associates.'

He recognized Diane's voice with relief. This would make it easier. 'Hello, Di, it's Riley.'

'Let me guess, sore tummy? Got the flu? Or maybe it's a fever that came on all of a sudden. A twenty-four-hour thing. The doctor said stay in bed.'

'Close. Toothache.'

'Ouch.'

'You said it. It's kept me up all night and I'm off to have it yanked.'

'Well, just take the whole day off honey, and even tomorrow if you have to.'

'Gee, thanks, Diane. I'll tell the boss you said so.'

'You do that and I'll deny all knowledge.'

'See you later.'

'Bye, Riley.'

Riley smiled. He liked Diane. He'd once got to the point of unbuttoning her blouse before she came to her senses and pointed out that her husband might object. With Jane, the other office girl, it was a different story. She was a sour-faced God-fearing bitch who would have ground his excuse to dust. It was good that Diane had answered. A good sign.

8.53 a.m. The taxi barely got above walking pace. For the most part hemmed in by slow-moving buses belching thick black diesel fumes. They still had a long way to go and it looked as if he was going to be late anyway.

'Isn't there another route we could take?'

The driver didn't even bother to turn his head, let alone answer. His thoughts drifted to his daughter. She would be on her way to school at this time. She looked cute in her little grey dress, her long brown hair tied back to stop it falling in front of her eyes when she bent over her desk. The teacher had told her it would ruin her vision and now she was too worried to ever wear it loose. But that was wrong. When he spoke to her two weeks ago she'd just had it cut. Really short. Just below the ears. He couldn't visualize her with short hair. Her face faded from his mind. He tried to bring the image of her back but couldn't. Instead he was stuck with the passing scenery. Uninspiring drab grey buildings weakly lit by the partially clouded autumn sun.

9.05 a.m. He ran along the corridor. Almost colliding with people carrying towers of paperwork. Their only objection being a raised eyebrow or slight frown. As he neared the door to room 712 he realized he was no longer angry but anxious. Anxious to have not done anything wrong.

The door to room 712 was open. A man hovered near a desk with his back to Riley, who coughed in a theatrical manner. The man spun round and flashed a smile. The effect was dazzling. A row of perfectly white and obviously capped teeth.

'You must be Mr Scott.' They shook hands. 'Please take a seat.'

'I was wondering,' Riley began, but the man raised his hand in a gesture to quieten him.

'I realize you want to get everything sorted out, but if you could just give me a couple of minutes so I can get this out of the way –' he touched some papers – 'then I'll give you my full attention.'

Feeling more at ease, Riley took a seat. The man had a friendly manner and 'the matter', as he had put it, couldn't be of much importance since he was plodding through his other work first. Riley watched him take out a fountain pen and start to scribble.

There was nothing to look at in the room. Plain white walls. No windows. No furniture except the two chairs and the metal desk between them. Indeed the only thing to admire in the room was the man himself and his immaculate appearance. Not one golden hair had been allowed to drift out of place. His attire an expensive work of art. The suit single-breasted. Three buttons. Dark rich-blue material. White shirt and dark tie. Gold cufflinks with red stones. Rubies. His nails rounded. Shining. Manicured. He struck Riley as more of an affluent playboy than a civil servant.

Riley studied his own nails. Bitten back and uneven. A habit he had tried to break many times. Especially when married. It was one of the numerous complaints his wife had had about him. She had hated to watch him nibbling in front of the television at night. Here and now he had the urge. Anything to use as a distraction.

Eventually the fountain pen was laid to rest and again Riley faced the dazzling smile.

'If we could establish a few facts first of all, then we can get down to the business in hand.'

'What business?'

'You are Mr William Riley Scott of flat 3, 8 Claremont Street?'

There was a pause. Riley said nothing. The man looked up at him. 'Is that correct?'

'I didn't realize that was a question. It is correct. What's your name?'

'Sorry?'

'You have an advantage on me. You know my name. I don't know yours.'

'It's irrelevant.' The man seemed flustered. 'Thompson. James Thompson.'

'Pleased to meet you, James. Carry on.' Riley felt pleased to have redeemed himself for his earlier misdemeanour of running in the corridor. Stupid thing to do. The worst he could get on a red light was a fine.

'You previously resided at 13 Manor Park before moving to your current address four years ago.'

'True.' Shit, it must be something to do with the divorce.

'You have of course been registered on the electoral roll during these past four years?'

'Yes.' Electoral roll? What the fuck?

'Have you executed your right to vote on occasion, Mr Scott?'

'Yes.'

'Has anyone to your knowledge used your vote or voted in proxy on your behalf?'

'No.'

Mr Thompson pushed a piece of paper towards him. 'Is this your signature?'

Riley pretended to look at the scrawl, but in his confusion he wasn't seeing anything. 'Yeah, I guess so.'

Mr Thompson stood with a smile of satisfaction. 'Good. Then it is my duty on behalf of His Majesty's Government to inform you that you have been selected at random from the electoral roll, in accordance with law, to actively participate in the execution of a death row inmate. You are legally required to make yourself available to the appropriate authorities for the next seven days or you will face prosecution. Do you understand?' Mr Thompson beamed as if he had just presented Riley with the keys to a new car.

'What?' was the only word Riley could form. The meaning of James's words slowly filtered through to him. It wasn't jury service. 'Execution'. 'Death row'. They echoed in his ears. Building louder and louder. A thunderstorm approaching. He tried to speak. To speak would drown them out. Break the spell. But he couldn't.

James nodded in sympathy. 'Obviously this has come as a shock to you.' The door opened and a girl entered carrying a tray. 'Ah, here's Sarah with the coffee.'

It was a mistake. Like he had said. Like Andrew had said. But a tiny glimmer of truth sparkled in Riley's soul and he knew there was no mistake. For an instant he was returned to the voting booth. A momentary hesitation before he put a cross in the box next to yes. Then signed. He remembered the argument in the bar the previous night. They were still mostly in their football kit, having rushed to the pub from a game of five-a-side. Stephen, fat, sweat pouring down his face, lager slopping over his red and white striped shirt. The team colours. Pointing an accusing finger at him. 'You wouldn't do it, so why expect someone else to?'

Riley and the others laughing. Gerald, who'd saved a penalty in the dying minutes of the game, thrusting his head between them. Answering for Riley. 'I'll push the button or string them up.' Everyone shouting, chanting. 'String them up. String them up. String them up.' Like a chorus from the terraces. Mitch the barman yelling at them to be quiet or they'd be out. Stephen later whispering in his ear, 'Think about it mate, 'cause if you vote yes tomorrow it could very well be you with your hands on the rope.'

He'd do it. He said he'd do it. But he wasn't the only one. They'd all said so. His breath was being sucked out of him and he could only manage a laboured whisper to the girl's question. 'Just black please.' She poured him a cup. He couldn't grasp the situation at all. He had just been asked to help kill a man and now the three of them were pleasantly discussing which biscuits to have. Chocolate chip or bourbon cream? Normally he would have been intent on her tits, which were amply exposed as she leaned across the tray. But her eyes consumed him and he knew he was pleading with her for help. She wouldn't understand. He didn't want to frighten her but he couldn't help himself. She handed him his drink with a serene smile. Seemingly unaware of his distress. Mr Thompson thanked her and she left.

'This can't be right.' A weak statement, but Riley knew he had to pursue it. Hold on to that thought. He must be able to argue his way out.

Mr Thompson shook his head sadly. 'I'm sorry Mr Scott, there is no mistake.'

'But...' Riley lost his words. He could think of nothing to say.

'There are no buts. You did vote in the referendum two years ago on capital punishment. You voted in favour of it and were fully aware of the terms and conditions of that vote. You knew that you might at some time be called into service in the event of an execution going ahead.'

'Well, I knew that was the basis of it.'

'Then there is no cause for complaint.'

'Complaint. For fuck's sake, you're asking me to murder someone.' Riley's hand trembled as he wiped the saliva from his chin. He had shouted. Anger surfacing. Taking him over. He had wanted to remain calm and logical but the fear was lurking inside now.

Mr Thompson remained impassive. 'No, Mr Scott, the state is asking you to fufil your civic duty.'

'It's insane. It's murder.'

'You didn't think so two years ago.'

'I don't care. I don't care what I thought two years ago. I can change, can't I?'

'In this case, no.'

'Well, I am.' He was adamant now. 'I am changing.'

'It seems to me, Mr Scott, that this thought did not cross your mind until today. Until it was you who was called forward. I think that had you been stopped on your way to work this morning and asked for your views on the death penalty, you would in all probability have still been in favour of it.'

'I don't give a shit what you think. I won't do it. No way.'

'Then you leave us with no alternative. We shall have to prosecute you.'

'Fine, I'll get my lawyer. Take me to court.'

Mr Thompson snorted.

Riley sprang to his feet. 'Don't fucking laugh at me.'

'I wasn't laughing. You clearly don't understand or wish to understand the situation. There won't be a trial. No judge or jury. You will simply be taken into custody and detained for a period of no less than ten years.'

An earthquake erupted inside Riley's head. The room started to spin. The ground slipped from his feet and he slumped back into his chair.

'You can't do that.'

'I'm afraid we can and certainly will, sir. It's the law.'

Silence. That was all he wanted. He put his hands over his eyes, wishing everything would disappear. Wishing to be in his bed. 7.49 a.m. Another ordinary day. He couldn't go to prison for ten years. All he'd done was put a cross in a fucking box.

'There must be some exceptions or right to appeal.'

'Indeed there are.' Mr Thompson shuffled through his papers. 'Let's see, have you suffered any form of mental illness at all?'

'No, but it's a distinct possibility for the future.'

'Are you or any close relatives suffering from a major or terminal illness?'

'No.'

'Have you been found guilty of any criminal act in the last two years?'

'No, you know I haven't, unless you include running a red light.'

'I'm afraid we don't.'

'No, I didn't think so.'

'So unless a close relative, such as your mother or father, were to die or fall ill in the next few days, I'm afraid you have no grounds for exemption.'

'What are you suggesting? That I murder my mother to get out of killing a stranger? Or perhaps I could just break her legs. Would that be enough?'

Riley started to giggle. Mr Thompson declined to join in the merriment. Couldn't he see the joke? What a fucking joke. For the first time since he was a five-year-old and had tumbled from a wall on to a concrete path, cracking his head, he felt the warm caress of tears running down his cheeks. He touched them in disbelief. 'What can I do?' he was asking Mr Thompson. 'What can I do?' He repeated the phrase several times until it died on his lips and he was left frozen. Unable to move or speak.

Mr Thompson stood up and came round from his desk. He crouched beside Riley, laying a comforting hand on his shoulder. 'Mr Scott, listen to me, or may I call you William?'

'Riley. Everyone calls me Riley.'

'Well, listen to me, Riley. I know this is the last thing in the world you expected. It's the last thing anyone expects, but it's in no way as disastrous as it seems. Yes, true, you have been selected to actively take part in an execution, but as it stands you are only one of three candidates. It is only at the end of an induction course that a final participant is chosen. So you see, there is already only a one in three chance that you will be called upon. You may not have to do anything at all. Then of course there may not even be an execution. It's true the prisoner has practically exhausted his right to appeal, but there are still a lot of options for a whole team of lawyers, experts and lobbyists to explore on his behalf. He may well have his sentence commuted.'

'Won't I just have to do the next one if that happens?'

'No, no.' Mr Thompson laughed easily. 'We couldn't operate on that basis and have ordinary citizens' lives disrupted indefinitely. Let me explain. Three candidates are chosen for each execution. Should the execution be postponed for a lengthy period or cancelled, then the three candidates are deemed to have fulfilled their civic duty and are not called on again.' James smiled reassuringly. 'I know it all sounds very dramatic when I read out the government spiel. I have to do that. It's my job. But believe me, there is nothing certain about the law. Nothing except should you refuse to take part, you will go to prison. I have seen it happen and you will receive scant sympathy.

'Look at it as if you're getting a little holiday. You have seven days to attend our course and in all probability you will not be requested to do anything further. Also, when the course is completed, you will be allowed seven days' leave from work funded by the government. Now that doesn't sound bad, does it?'

Riley nodded.

'Does it sound bad?'

'No. It sounds good.'

'Of course it does.' Mr Thompson returned to behind his desk. 'Now, we've been in touch with your office and informed them that you have been selected for jury service. So there's no need to worry about contacting anyone there and having to explain your absence.'

'Jury service?'

'It's a cover we use for the candidates' benefit. It can save an endless amount of embarrassment and future unpleasantness.' Mr Thompson appeared to think for a moment. 'May I give you some advice?'

'I could do with some.'

'I've found that the candidates who tend to cope best with this also tend to keep it quiet. You're not under any secrecy law or anything of that nature. It's just that friends' and relatives' reactions to your predicament can cause distress and unnecessary strain. So usually the fewer who know the better. Of course the press are severely restricted in this area. You need have no fear that your name or any private details will appear in the media. You are guaranteed anonymity. On no account will any journalist write a story about you. All clear?'

'Yeah, I suppose so.'

'Good.'

'Can I get some clothes and stuff from home?'

'Goodness gracious, Riley, we're not detaining you. What a terrible view you must have of the government. No, you will be free to live as normal while on the course.' He selected a file from his desk. 'There are just a couple of items left.' He extracted a sheet of paper from the file and laid it in front of Riley. 'This is your consent form. It requires your signature. It basically states that you have been informed of your circumstances and rights and have consented to fufil the requirements of the state.'

Mr Thompson uncapped his fountain pen and offered it to Riley, who reached out but didn't take it. He eventually withdrew his hand.

'I understand your hesitation, Riley. Obviously you need to think. There is in fact no need for you to sign your consent here and now. You have twenty-four hours to decide.'

Riley felt relief. Twenty-four hours, a chance to get hold of Andrew.

'I must have your signature by the time my office closes tomorrow. That's 5 p.m. If you haven't signed by then, you will be taken into custody. Do you understand?'

'Yes. I'd rather leave it just now.'

'That's fine.'

Riley rose. 'Is that all?'

'Not quite. I'm afraid I have to ask you to surrender your identity card. It's a precautionary measure just in case you get a silly notion and attempt to board a flight to a far-flung exotic destination. It will of course be returned to you at the earliest opportunity.'

Riley passed to Mr Thompson the small white card that each citizen was required to carry at all times. 'No sniggering at the picture.' It was one Riley hated. Taken when his hair had been much shorter. For some reason the camera had enlarged his ears to elephantine proportions.

'Ah, believe me, mine is no oil painting either.' Mr Thompson escorted him to the door. They shook hands. 'I shall see you tomorrow then?'

'Yeah.' Riley turned to go, then turned back. 'Can I ask a question, Mr Thompson?'

'Call me James.'

'The selection process, James, the final one, is it random?' James hesitated, then nodded yes. 'Then it doesn't depend on who does better or is more suited to the course?'

'I'm not really at liberty to discuss it, Riley. There's no marking system as such, so let's say it is called a random process.' James heavily emphasized the word random.

'So it's like you said, I'm just on the course. You could say I'm making up the numbers.'

'I've seen a lot of people come through this office in the past eighteen months, Riley, and I'm a pretty good judge. I think you'll be fine.'

'I'm making up the numbers.'

'That's right, Riley.' James winked. 'You're just making up the numbers.'

The Girl

At the entrance to the department of Justice and Corrections Riley joined the throng waiting for the rain to ease. He wondered if the other two candidates were here as well. Each unaware of the others' presence. Each cocooned in their own shell of disbelief. He doubted it. The people around him seemed at ease. No one appeared isolated. They chatted happily in low voices. Every now and then a group made a dart across the road or into a waiting taxi. Their only worry seemed to be what type of sandwich to have when lunchtime came around.

Riley shrank into a corner.

Maybe his reaction wasn't typical. Maybe some, when told they were to help kill a man, rejoiced. Were positively delighted to be of service.

From the arch spanning high above him hung a chandelier of crystal and brass. Its rays sparking across the gold letters encircling it. 'Peace Justice and Liberty'.

This made him laugh.

The question now was what could he do? He had to see Andrew and find a loophole. No matter how many hints Mr Thompson dropped or how much reassurance he offered, odds of three to one weren't good enough. A growing sense of helplessness coursed through his veins. What if there weren't any loopholes? When the government brought in the law they must have made it pretty watertight. Seventy-eight per cent had voted yes. Millions of people. Why him? Why the fuck him?

His bones ached. With the way he felt at the moment, he knew there was no sense in seeing Andrew. Without hope or heart that they could find an escape. If he was to have any chance of success he had to believe.

He couldn't face the emptiness of the flat. What he needed was a bar and a drink. He'd feel better after a drink. Then he'd call Andrew and see him in the afternoon.

He made his way outside with the speed and agility of a geriatric on the last mile of a marathon run. Someone banged into his shoulder and Riley clung to a stranger to stop himself careering head-first down twenty steps and smashing his skull on the pavement. He turned to curse the stupid bastard who had bumped into him but his profanities failed to materialize as he recognized the girl Sarah who had served him coffee. She was bent double, retrieving the contents of her bag. Sunglasses, keys, letters, balls of tissue littered the steps. Riley chased after her lipstick.

He managed to rescue it before it suffered beneath the wheels of a taxi. She met him at the bottom of the steps.

'I'm sorry. I almost knocked you off your feet. Are you all right?'

'I'm fine.'

'It's my own stupid fault for being in such a hurry.' He presented her with the lipstick. She gave him a mock curtsy. 'Thank you, kind sir.'

'You're welcome.' Riley wanted to tell her, 'They're making me kill someone.' He couldn't meet her eyes. He focused instead on a silver brooch pinned to the lapel of her black jacket. He was trembling. Suddenly aware that a dam was bursting inside. The fear rising uncontrollably. 'They're making me kill someone.' Another wave that made him feel sick. He bit his lip hard.

She put her hand on his. 'You're the man who was in with Mr Thompson, aren't you?'

'That's right.'

'He's a nice man, Mr Thompson.' She moved closer to him. The movement acted as a sedative to his troubled nerves. 'I'll let you into a secret.' He managed to look into her eyes. They were bright green. He hadn't noticed before, in the office. Their surface smooth. Almost liquid. As though nothing ever really disturbed them. Her pupils wide and dark. Riley wanted to dive into the darkness where he was sure it was warm and safe. 'There's some who work in there –' she indicated the building they had just left, its white stone streaked in shining stripes of rain – 'once they get behind a desk they go power crazy. They think that when they snap their fingers the world trembles. Not Mr Thompson. He's nice. I bet he treated you nice, didn't he?'

'I guess he did.'

'Of course he did.' She examined her watch. 'I better be running along. Nice to meet you again.'

'Nice to meet you, Sarah.'

'You remembered my name.' She sounded surprised. 'Do you mind if I ask you yours?'

'Not at all. Riley.'

'Goodbye, Riley. Who knows, we might bump into each other again.'

'I hope so.'

She grinned.

He watched as she walked off with a folded newspaper held above her head to stop her long black hair from getting wet from the fine spray of almost non-existent rain.

A quiet bar. Not flashy enough to attract the suit and tie

brigade. Riley preferred that. A place where the only coffee they served was filtered. No music. No theme. No fucking shamrocks stuck everywhere. He took a stool at the bar and sipped from his pint of cold gassy lager. The barman stood a few feet from him, enraptured in a game of South American football playing on a TV above the Gents' door. Riley guessed the twenty-two players were running around a field in Argentina since one of the sides was Boca Juniors. Normally he would have been as hypnotized as the barman.

'Do you have a newspaper?'

'Sure.' The barman peeled his eyes away from the screen long enough to pass a folded tabloid along to Riley.

The front page was full of the usual shit about the royal family. A subject that he and he guessed everyone else had long passed caring about. He remembered when one of them had died a few years ago and the whole country had suffered endless months of eulogizing. The TV, radio, papers, all had been saturated. It had been inescapable. Sickening. The woman in the flat above him had gone as far as to stick black bordering round her windows.

Who gave a fuck?

Page three was the standard bubbly blonde, except she was in her forties and celebrating twenty-five years of flaunting her tits to the nation. She wore a Union Jack top hat and the headline above proclaimed that 'Britain Loves Her Bouncers'. Riley almost ripped the paper to pieces in disgust.

The story he sought lay on page five. He knew that as the week progressed so would the story, to page one.

TIME RUNS OUT FOR HUGHES

Relatives of murder victim Nancy Sayer and their supporters cheered outside the High Court yesterday as an appeal to save the life of her killer, Tim Hughes, was rejected. In rejecting the appeal, Justice Lord Humphreys stated that there was insufficient evidence to warrant the granting of a new trial and that Mr Hughes's original conviction and sentence should stand.

Nancy's mother, Kerri (33), broke down upon hearing the announcement and said, 'He deserves to die for what he did. My daughter didn't have the choice to live or die. He took that choice from her. My life is a living hell and I won't have peace till I know that's where he is, burning in hell.'

Nancy (16), a popular girl in her hometown, disappeared on her way home after leaving a friend's house last August. Her body was discovered in nearby woods a week later. She had been beaten and raped before being strangled with a length of cord.

Mr Hughes (46), a local schoolteacher, was later arrested and convicted of the crime.

Hughes wasn't present in court to hear the decision. However, his lawyer, John Hubbard, QC, commented that there were still plenty of avenues open to his team and he felt confident that his client would not be executed on the given date.

Should the execution proceed this Sunday, Hughes will be the third man to lose his life to the death penalty since it was reinstated eighteen months ago.

Below the story was a picture of a middle-aged blonde with gold looped earrings and dark shadows beneath her eyes. She held a framed photograph of a young girl, also blonde. Next to the picture a quote, 'My Living Hell', and instructions to turn to page twelve.

Riley took a sip of his lager. He didn't care what 'hell' she was going through. He didn't want to be her avenging angel. He didn't care about her, her daughter or Tim Hughes. Why couldn't they just fucking leave him alone?

A man took the stool next to him. An elderly man with a straggly grey beard. He sighed with satisfaction after tasting his drink. 'Tastes good.'

Riley smiled out of politeness. 'Sure does.'

The man produced a packet of cigarettes. He eyed Riley. 'You don't mind, do you?'

'No, go ahead.'

'I know it's against the law, but me and my friend the barman have an arrangement to bend the rules now and then.'

'It's quite a rare sight these days, someone smoking.'

'Oh, there's still enough of us out there, puffing away. Being social pariahs, we just hide behind our doors. It's definitely changed, though, from when you were positively encouraged to light up. When a cigarette was guaranteed to give you the sex appeal and style of a Hollywood star. Apparently clean-living and hard work are the new government sponsored drugs.'

'I wonder why. Maybe no one wants to die any more. We'd rather have a vitamin pill, look frumpy and live for ever.'

The old man laughed. 'That could be it. No more heroes or outlaws. We're too busy trying to drag this living business out for as long as possible. You see, a cigarette is an instrument of social interaction.' He pointed to the barman. 'Nowadays we'd rather get that by watching television and have all our organs transplanted one by one. Although I know someone who doesn't want to live for ever.'

'Who?'

'That man.' He tapped the article in front of Riley.

'What do you mean? Do you know him?'

'No. I just remember that when he was originally sentenced to death he didn't want to appeal. He said he was ready to face his punishment. It was his wife who forced his lawyers into it.' The man gazed into the cigarette smoke curling into a cloud above him. 'Strange thing to want to die. I remember having the feeling once or twice myself. Strange thing he did. Maybe after something like that the only option you have is death. Unless you're one of these real cold-blooded bastards. Well, if it hadn't been for Mrs Hughes, he'd have got his wish. Been gone long ago. I wonder if he's grateful.'

Riley felt the sickness that had began inside Thompson's office returning. Cloying at his throat. The stale odour of the cigarette filled his lungs, turning his stomach even more. He finished his lager and slammed the empty glass on to the counter.

The old man didn't flinch, didn't seem to notice. Apparently lost in the thought of death. 'At least Mr Henderson will be a happy man.'

'Who?'

'Don't tell me you've forgotten Mr Henderson, he started all this. Don't you remember him camped outside the Home Office, starving himself until he was nothing much more than a sleeping bag of bones? I think he would have held out. I think he would have died if they hadn't given him his referendum. I guess when your only son walks out to get a paper two days before Christmas and doesn't come back, but is discovered in a basement of a house a few hundred yards from home, mutilated, sodomised, his killer only recently free after serving a sentence for previous attacks on children, justice would be on your mind.

The old man sucked in the last drags of his cigarette. He smiled. 'Maybe Hughes was just being considerate and trying to save us taxpayers a few pennies on the appeal.' His laughter degenerated into a rasping cough and he had to gulp at his drink to recover.

Riley glared at his sallow skin clinging to his skull, hanging lifelessly from his jawline. The burned-down cigarette clamped between bony fingers. 'You stupid old fuck. You'll cost the taxpayer just as much as he does when the cancer kicks in. It's just a question of who hits the grave first.'

The sunshine didn't cheer Riley at all. For a second he had caught the hurt expression on the old man's face before storming out of the bar. He cursed himself for sounding off. He had considered returning and apologizing, but the moment had passed.

'Good afternoon, Holden and Bernard.'

'Good afternoon, Susan.' Riley forced a cheerful note into his voice.

'If it isn't our Mr Scott. How are you today?'

'I'm fine, thank you, and yourself?'

'Counting the minutes till five. I presume you're in need of a good lawyer.'

'Your presumption is entirely correct.'

'I'm afraid you're out of luck. He's out.'

'Where?' Riley told himself not to panic.

'Stuttgart.'

'What the hell is he doing in Stuttgart? I spoke to him this morning and he said he'd be in the office all day.'

'That was the plan, but he got a call and had to go.'

'Fuck. I really need to speak to him. Can you give me a contact number?'

'No. He was supposed to ring us when he got there but so far hasn't. You could try his mobile. I have several times but it's been switched off. Probably still is, you know how he likes to hide.'

'You must have contact with him. We're living in the age of quick and easy global communication, for Christ's sake. Who was he visiting? Where was he staying? There must be a fax number or an e-mail.'

'Keep calm, Riley.'

'I really need to speak to him. It's urgent.'

'I haven't got a number at the moment. If it's a crisis, then you can always see someone else from the firm.'

'No, it has to be Andrew.'

'If he calls I'll get him to call you, but failing that he's back tomorrow. Although he's got a very full day.'

'You'll have to fit me in, Susan. It's important.'

She chuckled. 'How important?'

Riley relaxed. He knew what she was after. 'Are we talking truffles?'

'Mmmmmmm.' A cat purred on the end of the line.

'Chocolate-coated?'

'Plain chocolate.'

'Of course. Half a pound?'

'It's a deal. The best I can give you is 3 o'clock.'

'Can't you make it earlier? I need it earlier.'

'He's back at 12. Due in court at 1. I can give you half an hour by shunting someone else aside. That's a very good offer.'

'I know and I love you for it, Susan.'

'I love you too, Riley. Tomorrow at 12.15.'

Riley nestled the phone into its cradle. Buses thundered past him, their roar dulled by the Perspex of the call box. Someone had scratched the word cunt into the panel facing the road. Exactly, Riley thought, Stuttgart. Unbelievable. He opened the door and quickly escaped from the aroma of stale urine.

The school bell rang and a few minutes later the kids began to spill out of the wrought-iron gates. He saw his daughter before she saw him. Skipping along with her bag in one hand and, despite the chill, her coat in the other. The new haircut almost turned her into a stranger. A face he vaguely recognized. Someone he used to know who had moved on to another life. The sadness overwhelmed him as he realized how much he missed her. Missed seeing her grow. Perhaps he was more susceptible after the morning's events but once more he felt tears in his eyes.

She broke into a sprint at the sight of him and jumped into his arms. He hugged her tight.

'Dad Dad Dad Dad,' she chanted at him.

'Look at the state of your coat.' In her eagerness to reach him, she had dragged her coat along the ground. The bottom of it and one of the sleeves were now streaked with dirt and stuck with leaves. Riley tried to wipe it clean.

'Your mother will kill me for that.'

'I didn't know you were picking me up today.'

'I'm not. I had the afternoon off work, so I thought I'd come and see how my favourite girl is getting along.' They rubbed noses. 'How are you?'

'I'm fine.' She squinted at her thumb and held it in front of him for inspection. 'Although I split my thumbnail and the teacher had to cut it back for me and now it's really sore.'

Riley popped the thumb into his mouth. She giggled and pulled it out.

'Better?' he asked.

'No.'

'Or maybe ice cream would make it better.'

'Ice cream,' she whispered excitedly.

'Hello, stranger.' It was Anne. He straightened up and faced her. She too had had her hair cut. Her long blonde hair now in a bob.

'Hi.'

'What are you doing here?' Her voice was cold. She ignored Emma, who was hopping on the spot and tugging at her sleeve.

'Mum, can we get ice cream?'

'Quiet a minute, Emma.'

'But ice cream, Mum.'

'We don't have time, honey. You've got tap in half an hour.'

'Oh.' Emma's face crumpled and she fell into a sulky silence.

Anne stared at Riley. 'I asked you what you're doing here.'

'I got the afternoon off work so I thought I'd drop by.'

'It's better if you phone first if you want to pick her up from school.'

'It was on the spur of the moment.'

'I wanted ice cream.' Emma said it with a tinge of a whine in her voice.

'I'm sorry, girl. I didn't know you had tap. We'll do it another time.'

'Sunday maybe,' Anne said.

'Sunday?'

'It's your day this week.'

'Is it?'

'Yes. You were supposed to have her a fortnight ago but you bowed out. Again.'

'Yeah. OK.' Riley smiled at Anne weakly.

The look that Anne gave him was one of complete contempt. She took Emma's hand. 'Come on, honey, we have to get going.'

Riley watched their disappearing figures. Every now and then his daughter turned to wave goodbye. It reminded him of the day they had left to stay with a friend of Anne's for what was termed 'a break'. Emma had turned and waved that day as well. She had asked him where Mummy was taking her and he had replied, 'On a mystery tour.' Three weeks later they had returned and it was Riley's turn to pack his bags. Now she was going home. He'd meant to tell her he'd got the letter but it was too late.

On his way home he passed a street vendor selling the evening paper. Attempting to catch the attention of the workers battling each other and the hazards of public transport by screaming at them, 'Killer still to die.' Riley bought himself a bottle of whisky for company.

The Coke ran out before the whisky so Riley had to settle for it neat. He swallowed a mouthful and his face contorted. In the movies they drank neat whisky without visible signs of distress. It burned all the way down to his guts. Half a bottle already had him in a severe sweat. It meant he wasn't a real man. Real men drank neat whisky. He swallowed some more and had trouble getting it past his larynx. He broke into a fit of coughing.

The telephone rang. He considered answering in case it was Andrew. He'd tried his mobile several times but it remained switched off. He was still debating whether to answer or not when his machine clicked on. He listened to himself intently.

'Yes, you've guessed it, nobody here. Leave a message and I'll get back to you.'

The tone of his voice was weedy and shrill. I don't even sound like a man, he concluded.

A female voice screamed out into the digital recording. 'The roast is nothing more than ashes and I've just finished two bottles of very good-quality wine. You bastard, Riley.'

In his fury he hurled his glass at the buzzing tone. It curved through the air gracefully. Bouncing off the target and rolling underneath the television.

'Fuck off, Clara,' he shouted at his machine. 'Just fuck off. Who cares about your fucking roast? You're not even a decent fucking cook. I don't care. Nobody fucking cares.' He leaned over on his hands and knees. Face inches from the square black box of the answering machine to emphasize his point. 'Nobody fucking cares.' He scrambled to his feet and found another glass in a cupboard in the kitchen. He changed his mind and drank from the bottle.

Real men drank from the bottle.

The Lawyer

Some swine had sneaked up on Riley while he was asleep and glued his eyes together. He finally managed to prise them open. He was looking at his living room from a rather unusual angle. Pain shot through the right side of his face and seized his jawbone. Sand seemed to be settled in the back of his throat and he couldn't swallow. Something he badly wanted to do. It would maybe help him get rid of the sharp acrid taste that coated his teeth and had crystallized around the edges of his mouth.

His nose was blocked. His fingers explored his nostrils and encountered hard black snot. He scraped it out and breathed. The air smelled stale. It finally filtered into his consciousness that he was lying on the floor. He tried to lift his head and found it to be a battle. The movement dislodged a delicately balanced rock of nausea from its resting place and sent it crashing through his skull. Sharp needles jabbed behind his eyeballs. His stomach contracted. He clamped his teeth together but bile escaped through his lips and seeped down his chin. Riley swallowed the rest back. Gagging in the effort. His guts didn't react kindly to this turn of events and kicked even harder to empty its contents. Riley crawled at high speed to the toilet and puked into the bowl. The liquid was dark yellow and sunk in blobs to the bottom of the water. For a moment he basked in the warm glow of well-being after puking. Then the fever in him broke and he was left shivering. Sweat sticking to a forehead clouded with a deep throbbing. He puked once more then flushed. The sight of the clean sparkling toilet made him feel better. All the sickness taken away. He stripped off and got under the shower. Not standing upright but huddling on his knees. Letting the hot water scald his back. Massage his ills.

He lay on the sofa with a cup of coffee and learned from the mid-morning news that Tim Hughes had another appeal being heard today. Riley silently prayed.

Beside him was a letter. A reminder from the Department of Justice and Corrections that he had to call by their offices before 5 o'clock.

On his way out of the door he dumped the near-empty whisky bottle into the bin. An end to self-pity, he thought. From now on he would take control of events.

'Haven't you forgotten something?' Susan held her hand out in a demanding fashion.

Riley's head still hurt and he wasn't particularly in the mood for the stupid charades she liked to play. 'I forgot.'

She nibbled the end of her pen furiously and a frown appeared. 'That's very naughty.' She caught on to the fact that he didn't want to join in the game and relented. 'But I'll forgive you. Just this once.' She said it sternly.

He took her hand and squeezed it appreciatively. 'Thanks, Susan.'

It was her hands that first attracted him to her. Her long thin fingers. Each one the bearer of a large silver ring. Even her thumbs. Nails black and shiny. He still liked to imagine them digging into his arse as he fucked her.

He had indeed fucked her on one occasion. When she had enticed him to her home after a drunken office party. He couldn't remember anything about it except she had played some terrible ambient music the entire night that sounded like several whales groaning in distress and had given him a happy pill for stimulation. Neither mentioned it now and she never indicated she was ready for a repeat performance.

'You can go straight in, Riley.'

Andrew greeted him with a sunny 'Hello.' The office didn't suit him. Neither did the large wooden desk that his feet were propped up on. His appearance was that of a child masquerading as an adult. The dark pinstripe suit, black brogues, shirt and tie, contrasted with the baby face. Smooth skin that a pimple had never blemished. A chin that required shaving about twice a year. Soft, round, half-formed features. He had tried to combat this by growing a prominent sleek quiff and sideburns, and by puffing on cigars. Riley found the effect fascinatingly grotesque. The sideburns were a poor effort. Little tufts of pre-pubescent hair that sprouted near his ears. When he lit a Havana, eyes that betrayed the intelligence inside the child's body bulged almost to the point of popping from their sockets as he sucked in smoke. It made Riley cringe in the way he had done when he first heard his mother swear.

'So what's the trouble? Susan told me you were in distress when you called. Was it that meeting you had?'

'Yes.' Riley nibbled on his thumbnail. 'Tim Hughes.'

'Who?' Andrew's face was blank for a moment. 'Oh, the poor fellow facing the drop. What about him?'

'That's why they wanted to see me.'

Andrew seemed puzzled. 'Why would they choose you as a witness?'

'Not a witness.'

'Then what?' Riley saw the spark ignite in Andrew's eyes. 'Good God, no. It can't be.'

'Yes. They want me to help him, as you put it, take the drop.'

'Good God. Why?'

35

'Selected at random from the electoral roll.'

'It's amazing.' Andrew's grin split his face in half.

'I want out, Andrew. Not congratulations.'

'Of course you do. Forgive me. It's just it's rarer than meeting someone who has won the lottery.'

'I'd rather have had the prize with the cash.'

'Tell me the whole story.'

Riley related the events of the day before while his friend took notes.

Sitting in the oak-panelled office, he started to feel a sense of security. Something he hadn't done since he had opened the letter the previous morning. A knowledge that everything would work out all right.

'So you didn't sign the form?'

'No. He said I had until 5 o'clock today.'

'I don't know much about this. I haven't encountered it before.' Andrew smiled at him. 'Don't worry. I know a man who does.' He dialled a number. 'The first thing is to find out about the form.'

Riley wandered round the office feigning interest in the certificates on the walls but all the while hooked on the conversation behind him.

'Hello, Charlie, it's Andrew here. Fine. Couldn't be better. And you? Excellent. Listen I have a query for you, it's the death penalty. You know how members of the public have to take part now. Yes. That's right. What are they called? Why? No, I've never heard of it. I've got one in my office right now. Don't get so excited, Charlie. Anyway, it's about the consent forms they have to sign. Do they affect their status or have any legal ramifications should they choose to withdraw? I see. What about exemptions?'

Riley concentrated on the mass of grey clouds confronting him from the window. He waited for a ray of sunshine. Believing, like a child, that if he wanted it hard enough it would come. From Andrew. Not from the sky. Exemption.

'I see. What's his name?' Riley turned and saw Andrew jotting down more notes on to his pad. 'OK. Thanks, old son. Sure, that would be splendid. I'll relieve you of some more of your cash. Give me a ring.'

'Anything?'

'Nothing new. If you sign the form and pull out afterwards you'll just end up in the clink, same as if you hadn't signed. It's used as an ultimatum to get their ball rolling so to speak. So my advice is to sign while I get on with getting you out. I'm in court all afternoon but I'll have a couple of my lieutenants get right on the case.'

'But by signing, won't it be showing a willingness on my part?'

'You already demonstrated that at the ballot box. They're not interested in whether you're happy or not, Riley, they just want to get it done. The main thing is to keep you free and your options open.'

'There is a way out, though, isn't there? The guy I spoke to said there wasn't.'

'There's always a way out. His job isn't to help you, it's to get you on the programme. What did you say his name was?'

'James Thompson.'

'Never heard of him. Describe him.'

'About my age. Blond hair. Very dapper. Expensive suit and a suntan.'

'Sounds familiar. I know a few names over there, so I'll get on to them.'

'People who owe you favours?'

'It's a useful thing, being able to call in a few debts. My friend Charlie, for instance, he's given me the name of a man who's a specialist in this field. So I'll give him a ring. Speaking of names, did you know that you have a name in the legal jargon?'

'What do you mean?'

'You and the other candidates. You're known as the 18th Pale Descendants.'

'Why?'

Andrew shrugged. 'Fucked if I know, Riley. Some of these civil servants tend to be of the old school. It's probably some private joke in the halls of Eton or something like that.' He checked the time. 'Shit. I really have to get to court.'

He walked with Riley into the reception area. Past the potted plants and abstract art. 'Don't worry. I'll sort this mess out. But, you know –' his voice dropped and it was as if he was talking to himself – 'it is, in its way, a one in a million opportunity.' He switched his attention back to Riley. 'Can I ask you a question?'

'Of course.'

'What do you think of Tim Hughes?'

'I don't understand.'

'Do you think he should hang?'

It was a question Riley had denied asking himself. Afraid of the answer. Afraid of the truth. 'I don't know enough about the case.' The reply sounded lame.

'Yes, but in principle?' Silence. 'Because, you know, you put him in this position. You voted for it.'

Riley continued to say nothing.

'Ah, Susan, how's my favourite receptionist?'

Susan glared at them.

'Riley, what have you been doing to Susan?'

'He forgot my chocolates.'

Dominic tutted. 'You have to take care of Susan, Riley. Without her goodwill you may never see me again.'

The route from Andrew's office to Clara's house couldn't be termed scenic or quick. Run-down 1960s office blocks petering out into wasteland that eventually sprouted terminally boring semi-detached houses with front and back gardens. It was also a good four miles, but he decided to walk, being in no hurry to get there. Reluctant to see her but knowing he had to. Knowing he would feel better for getting it out of the way.

The slight confidence he had built during the meeting with Andrew deserted him. He kept his head down. Felt tense when passing someone in the street. Stupid of course. Nobody knew. But that didn't matter.

He reached a cluster of shops. An oddity from the past. A high street from an old town that had long ago been swallowed by the city. The row of pebble-dashed shops contained a newsagent's, an off-licence and a hairdresser's with the name Chique emblazoned above its window in orange plastic and bold black lettering. The final shop was an electrical store. Vaughan's. Riley stopped. Caught by the televisions in the window and the face framed behind the newscaster, the word below the picture, APPEAL.

The photograph was blurred and all Riley could make out of Hughes was a healthy tan, deep-set eyes and long silver hair.

Once inside, a girl approached him. 'Can I help you, sir?'

'No. I'm just browsing.' The sound from the televisions was barely audible. 'Actually, can you turn it up? I need to hear it.'

'Of course, sir. This set uses the latest in digital audio technology. It will link you with the latest cable or satellite systems and is a user-friendly gateway to the Internet. I don't know if you noticed, but we have a special sale on at the moment.'

The girl continued to speak, but Riley never heard a word. The picture changed to that of a man clutching a briefcase and trying to leap his way through a pack of journalists. His head darting in several directions in an attempt to answer the barrage of questions. Mainly the same question. His reply was caught by the microphone just as he managed to squeeze through some doors.

'Yes, we do expect a successful conclusion.'

Riley guessed this to be John Hubbard, Hughes's lawyer.

The picture cut to the reporter. Raincoat. Hair blowing wild in the wind. A brass plaque declaring him to be outside the High Court.

'For three hours the legal team for Mr Hughes appealed for his life. The hearing, heard before three judges and headed by Lord James Struthers, is the final chance for convicted killer Hughes to have his death sentence commuted by a court. Should this fail only Parliament and the Home Secretary could save him from the gallows. The feeling in the public gallery and from the Hughes legal team was that the impassioned plea for clemency came over extremely well and in every likelihood it will be granted. So although a judgement may not be received until this evening, it seems that Tim Hughes will not be the third man to be hanged since the reinstatement of the death penalty but the first to escape it.'

The end of the report was lost to Riley as a barrage of fireworks exploded in his head. It's all off. It's all off. Jesus, thank you. It's all off. He became aware that the shop assistant, who had moved away a slight distance, was staring at him, but he continued to look at the screen even though the report had changed. As if disbelieving what he had heard and seen.

Aerial shots of a green forest with an ugly black scar across it. Pieces of wreckage visible like confetti on a pavement after a wedding. Pleasure beamed all over his face. One hundred and forty-three dead.

'Are you all right, sir?' She touched his arm. A gesture of concern but her eyes were wary. A nutter in the shop was her obvious thought.

Riley saw her name-tag. Her long auburn hair. Hazel eyes. Small mole beneath the right eye.

'I'm fine, Natasha.' She blushed slightly. 'I'm fine.'

'So didn't you think you were taking a bit of a chance coming round here? Alex could have been home from work or sometimes John comes back for lunch from school.'

'I decided it was worth the risk.'

'The way I feel now I couldn't agree more.' She lay on her back beside him. Naked. Hands behind her head. He reached out and took hold of her breast. Squeezed. She smiled.

She had frowned when he knocked on the door. He had never known an urge like it. The power inside him. Before she could protest, complain, vent her anger at him, he had her bent over her dining-room table. Knickers cast aside on the floor. He then took her upstairs to do the same thing again. Only more leisurely. Taking time to do all the little things she liked.

'You should have phoned me. Said there was an accident with your daughter. I wouldn't have been angry.'

He avoided her look of concern. 'I know. I just panicked and ran off to the hospital.'

'I'd have understood that. I know how important kids are.'

'Anyway, the main thing is she's going to be all right, and you're happy as well.'

'You bet I am.' She sighed and stretched.

This was a pose he liked to study her in. Her legs bent so he could enjoy the curve of her thighs and calves. Arms raised, lifting her breasts. She hadn't changed all that much in the seventeen years since he had first seen her. He was fourteen when she and her husband moved into the house next door. The new neighbours hadn't registered with Riley until one morning in the summer holidays when he rose and discovered her through his bedroom window. Sunbathing in the back garden. Her dark blue bikini undone. Folded down. Barely covering her nipples.

Even now he felt there was a surreal quality to them being together. A full eight months after he had bumped into her in the supermarket and she had invited him to the house for coffee. Both knowing in that instant that they wanted more than coffee. For two years the figure of her lying there had been his fantasy. Daily he had stood by the window. Hypnotized by every movement of her body. Masturbating at the thought of being with her. He had gathered together the courage to buy a porn magazine he had seen in a newsagent's with a woman resembling her on the front cover. The same pouting mouth and long dark curly hair. At nights, in bed with the magazine, he could almost believe she was there with him.

He was sure she knew he watched her. She smiled at him knowingly when they spoke. Brushed against him once in the local shop. Eventually he left home for university. Returning on holiday after the first term, his parents threw a New Year's party. The neighbours filling the house. Including Clara and her husband. Watching her sink back countless gin and tonics and flit from guest to guest in her short blue dress, he realized his fixation, despite the gropings with female students and lost virginity, had only intensified. When their eyes met, she smiled her knowing smile.

After the celebration of midnight and the ringing of the bells, he stood in the dark by his bedroom window. Staring at the streetlights and the houses containing thousands of parties. He heard her come in but didn't turn round. She put her arms around his waist. Pressed herself into his back. He could smell the gin from her breath and the synthetic odour of her hairspray. She dropped her hands to his crotch. Unbuttoned his jeans. Took out his cock and wanked him off. The only thing she said before walking out was 'Happy New Year.'

Even now the memory sent a tingle into his loins.

Riley checked the time. 3.30 p.m.

'I better be going.'

'What time does visiting start?'

'At 4.'

'You better get a taxi. Do you want me to call one for you?'

'That would really give the curtain twitchers round here

something to talk about. I'll go to the main road and get one.'

'I suppose you're right.' Clara got out of bed and started to dress. Riley busied himself with his own clothes. Avoiding the sight of her. The sag of her stomach and breasts. The folds of skin. It was at moments like these, and when he kissed her with his eyes open, saw the deep lines around her eyes or noticed the wrinkles on her hands when she touched him, that he wondered what the fuck he was doing. 'I might be able to arrange to have Friday night free.'

'Why don't you give me a call when you know?'

'OK.'

He searched his pockets. 'Shit, is the bank down the road still open?'

'No. It closed years ago. Why?'

'I haven't got the money for the taxi fare on me. I meant to get some out earlier but I forgot.'

Clara took some notes from her purse and pressed them into his hand.

'Take that.'

'Are you sure? I'll give you it on Friday.'

'Friday.'

Riley closed his eyes and they kissed.

He paused at the gates of the house next door. His old house. Only slight changes had occurred to the place in the passing years. The iron gates were white instead of black and the fern bushes his dad had planted in each corner of the garden were gone. Replaced by ornate miniature trees. The driveway had been repaved and a shiny dark green four-door sat proudly where his dad's ancient Triumph Dolomite had once been installed.

Ever since the break with Anne, their relationship had turned awkward. They couldn't seem to forgive him for damaging their happiness and instilling in them the fear of losing their grandchild. They had barely spoken in two years. No Christmas cards. No birthday cards. He remembered the shock when he had last seen his dad. How much he had aged. All he had wanted to do was to put his arm around him.

The elevator shuddered to a halt at the third floor. Two men got out. One girl got in. A girl with long black hair. Riley tapped her on the shoulder.

'Hello, Sarah.'

'Hello, Riley. How are you?'

'I'm doing great. Up amongst the clouds today.' He was pleased she had recognized him and remembered his name. It meant he had made some sort of impression on her. 'How about yourself?'

'Not too good. I could be in for a bit of a caning.' She tapped the files she held. 'I was supposed to have these on the boss's desk twenty minutes ago but I got chatting to the girl in the records office and time just flew.'

'Surely our benign Mr Thompson won't be that harsh?'

'Oh, he'd be sweet. Unfortunately, it's not him I'm reporting to today.' The floor lurched and they bumped shoulders as the elevator ground to a halt. 'I hate getting in this thing. When you go down it drops so fast you feel as if your stomach is still a few floors above you and your feet go numb. I always think I'm going to get stuck in it.' They both got out on the seventh floor. 'A couple of people did last summer. It took six hours to get them out.' She pointed to her right. 'I go this way. Is that who you are seeing, Mr Thompson?'

'Yeah.'

'Well, good luck.' She spun her foot on her heel and swivelled her hips slightly but still didn't move off.

Riley found his hands straying into his jacket pockets and when his voice came it stumbled in his throat. Emerging as no more than a croak.

'I'm sort of in your debt really.'

'How do you make that out?'

'You served me coffee the last time I was here so I feel I should return the favour. I could buy you a cup after work.'

'That would be nice. I finish in an hour.'

'I could meet you downstairs.'

'OK. I'll see you then.'

As she disappeared along the corridor, Riley wondered how stupid he looked with the large silly grin that was plastered on to his face. Thirty-one years old and he still found it a killer, without alcohol, to ask a girl for a date. He tried to adjust his thoughts as he approached room 712, but then shrugged off the attempt. Why bother? There was nothing to worry about any more.

'Welcome aboard.'

Riley shook the hand that was offered to him. Mr Thompson sank back into his chair with an air of ease and well-being. He glanced at the form Riley had just signed before putting it into a desk drawer. As before he was dressed with distinction. A grey single-breasted suit, white shirt. Sharp creases and a starched collar. As if he had just stepped from the pages of a magazine and stress was a word he had never heard of.

'When it reached 4, I wasn't sure if you had tried that flight to Rio or not.'

'It did cross my mind.'

'I can't blame you for that. There's a couple of administrative details that I have to inform you of before you go. A car will call for you at 8.30 tomorrow morning. It will take you to the instruction course, then return you afterwards at 5. Lunch is provided.'

'Where is the course held?'

'I'm not exactly sure. Somewhere in the city.'

'What does it consist of?'

'All I have on that is a statement which says "Instruction in the Theory and Practicalities of State Execution".'

'Does that include rehearsals?'

'I would assume so. However, I really have no idea. Do you have any other questions?'

'I want to know how to claim expenses. I've had to get a couple of taxis here and it's been quite costly.'

'An expense sheet will be given to you after you have completed your time with us and you will be recompensed in due course. If that's all.'

Riley rose to leave.

'You seem a lot calmer, more upbeat compared to yesterday.'

'I think the shock of it has worn off a bit now. It still gives me the jitters, but I guess I can cope. I thought about what you said and you're right, nothing is certain yet.'

'And you've been watching the news. The appeal.'

'Have they made an announcement yet?'

'No. It's not expected until late tonight. It's very unusual for a judgement to take so long.'

Riley sensed that Mr Thompson could have said more. 'Have you heard any whispers?'

'Preparations by our department are going ahead as normal. Although not with what you would call expedition.' He raised one eyebrow. 'If you get my drift.'

'I do, Mr Thompson.'

They sat at a corner table in the café. Sarah delicately manoeuvred the last piece of cake on to her fork and gently lifted it to her mouth. As the fork emerged from between her lips minus the cake, she gave a sigh. Riley laughed.

'What's funny?' she asked.

'You.'

'Oh, but, God, it's delicious.' She dabbed with a napkin at the crumbs stuck to her chin. 'When I first got the job at DJC

I used to come in here every lunchtime and inevitably I'd plump for one of their French cakes. After a few weeks plump was an understatement for the shape of me. I expanded at an alarming rate. So I cut down and now it's only birthdays and anniversaries. Special occasions.'

'Is this a special occasion?'

'Of course.'

'So what anniversaries do you have?'

'Unfortunately, there are quite a few. My mum and dad's wedding. I like to celebrate on their behalf in here. The day I became a godmother to my sister's daughter. The day I started work. The day Yuri Gagarin was launched into the stars. Edmund Hillary reached the summit of Everest. India became an independent nation. There's simply thousands, but at least it isn't every day now. I have some restraint.'

'Do you want another coffee?'

She pushed her cup to the centre of the table. 'No. I'm coffee'd out.'

He reached and touched her hand. 'Are you sure?'

'Yeah.' She didn't withdraw but left her hand there. Playing with the pepper pot. Attempting to balance it on top of the salt shaker. 'My mum will kill me. I'll never be able to eat all my dinner now.'

'Do you stay with your parents?'

'Of course. We all need a bit of guidance now and then to stop us straying from the proper path and it's handy to have that close by. I suppose you're in a bachelor pad.'

'I wouldn't call it a pad.'

'Where you take all your girls.'

'What girls?'

She didn't answer. Instead she peered hard at the pepper pot as it wobbled on the tiny spout of the salt shaker. She carefully took her fingers from it. For a second it balanced, before falling. It rolled in a curve to the edge of the table and Riley caught it as it dropped.

'Is that what you want me to be, Riley, one of your girls?'

The same feeling as before, when he'd asked her for coffee. An awkwardness. He forced himself to meet her gaze. Her bright emerald-green eyes.

'No. If I was asking you anything it would be to be the one girl. The only girl.'

'I should bloody think so as well.' She grinned at him. 'I'm going to powder my nose, or should I be truthful and say I'm going for a piss?'

'Always tell the truth. That's my philosophy.'

'See you in a minute.'

He drained his cup. This felt good. Really good. In fact, if he was being honest, except for a girl he'd briefly met on a train journey about a year ago, he'd never felt the electricity with anyone since Anne. He remembered that girl almost every day. They'd chatted for a couple of hours before she'd walked off into the crowded station. But he felt the charge now. Strongly.

The café was busy. Hardly a free table. An old man faced Riley a few feet away. Picking his way through a leafy salad. Their eyes met. Riley half smiled in acknowledgement. His face seemed familiar. The neatly trimmed beard and silver hair swept back. Shining healthy features. Riley couldn't put a name to him.

He glanced idly through the menu at all the things he could have to eat now his appetite was returning. Chilli cheeseburger, lemon chicken with olives. He'd get a take-away to scoff at home.

'I know a man who wants to die.' The old guy in the bar. Only his beard was straggly and he had a cigarette clamped between his fingers. The rasping cough.

'It can't be.'

'What can't it be?' The returning Sarah blocked his view.

'Nothing.' He strained to see round her. By the time he managed it, the table had been vacated. All that remained was a plate containing a few limp green leaves, a used and ruffled napkin and an empty glass.

'What is it, Riley?'

'It's me going mad.' It couldn't have been him. He stood up. 'Shall we go?'

'Yeah.' She laid a hand on his shoulder. Kissed him on the cheek. 'Thanks for the coffee.'

Riley waited at the counter to pay. Thoughts of the old man had been dispelled. He felt good again. Really good. The girl passed him the bill. He found some money in his trousers. Took out the notes. He vaguely wondered why the money wasn't in his wallet as usual, then remembered. Notes Clara had given him. He dropped them on the counter as if they burned his hand. He wondered why the world couldn't just fuck off and leave him alone for a night.

'Keep the change.'

The girl beamed at him. 'Thank you, sir.'

According to the news, there'd been a further delay and the result of the Hughes appeal wouldn't be known until tomorrow. An interview with a psychologist revealed that the man himself was likely to be feeling a certain amount of strain tonight and might not sleep well.

What an insight, Riley thought.

He'd left Sarah at a bus stop. She'd promised to see him again. He stripped off and got into bed. Tomorrow he'd find out about death. The practicalities of killing a man. At least that was as close as he would get and if the reprieve came early he might not even get that far.

The fluorescent lights hurt his eyes. Blinded him as they passed above his head. He fought with all his strength against the two men, dark hulking shadows that dragged him along the corridor. Their nails dug into his wrists. The sockets of his arms flashed with pain as he was pulled and twisted. The floor was of no help to him. It too hurt his eyes. The sheer whiteness of it hurt him to look at. Despite its tiled appearance each time he tried to use it for leverage, his foot disappeared beneath its surface. Radiating ripples and a shimmer of light. As if someone was sending him a message with a mirror via the sun. His feet became chilled. Nor was the floor smooth but a milky powdered glass that scraped his back. Cut into him.

They reached a metal door, which the two men swung open. They went through. Another corridor. The same painful light. They moved faster. Another door. Another corridor. Faster. Layer upon layer of skin stripped from him. Another door. Each one increased the panic he felt inside. He started to scream, then found he couldn't stop. Another door. Another corridor. Still faster. Another door. They stopped. The two men hauled him to his feet. He stood on the edge of an impenetrable blackness. He couldn't tell if it was solid or a gaping hole. The two men were gone. There seemed to be nothing to stop him turning round. Retreating. But he could feel invisible hands holding him to that spot. He could only go forward. He took a step, felt a rush of icy wind and plunged into the darkness.

Riley realized the noise he could hear was his own voice bursting from his lungs. He closed his mouth. Became aware he was sitting upright in bed. Sweating. Trembling. He took a sip of water, almost dropping the glass in the process, and collected his duvet from the floor. After a few deep breaths he rested his head on the pillow. Closed his eyes. Felt two men grab his arms. His eyes snapped open.

4 a.m. He drew his legs to his chest. Hugged himself. Lay watching the time pass. Waiting for the sun to rise. Morning. When he would be safe again.

The Murder

He sank into the soft black leather of the car's interior. The
driver had insisted on him sitting in the back and been rather
cool when Riley tried to make conversation. They had swiftly
left the city and were doing a steady ninety on the motorway.
The passing bushes and trees soon bored him. He also felt
slightly embarrassed that his friendliness towards the driver had
all but been rebuffed. He stared at the back of the man's head.
He was about fifty, with short steely grey hair and a neatly
trimmed moustache. Riley had noticed that his tie clip bore a
military insignia, but which corps or regiment it represented
was a mystery to him. He thought it a good opener, a bit of chat
would have helped pass the journey, but he knew it wasn't to
be. His stare must have carried weight and touched a nerve, for
the man flinched and looked at Riley in his rear-view mirror.
Riley pretended not to notice and let his gaze wander out of
the window. They passed a coach. Empty except for the driver.

An hour to their destination. A prison barge anchored two
miles off the coast. Riley closed his eyes.

The morning news reported that an announcement on the
Hughes appeal was scheduled for noon. Andrew hadn't
phoned. It worried him. Andrew was sure to have got an
inkling of the result.

The car shuddered and Riley woke. It took a moment for him to orientate himself. They were the only vehicle on the deck of a ferry. The ramp they had just descended was already drawn up and they were moving. He rubbed at his neck, which had stiffened.

'Is it OK to stretch my legs?'

'They prefer you to stay in your car, but I guess they can't stop you if you won't. The crossing only takes ten minutes.'

Riley got out. The ferry stank of oil and diesel tangible enough for him to feel it was coating his tongue. The sort of smell that was guaranteed to quickly make him nauseous. He strolled to the side railing. Below, the sea was black. The crest of the waves created by the ferry a dull grey. Ahead he could see the prison. It looked like a large tanker with enormous containers on deck. Which in effect it was. Only the cargo being human and going nowhere. Behind, there rose cliffs. A few houses were visible in the inlet from where they must have boarded. Above, seagulls followed the boat. Some circling the twirling navigational mast. Riley stared at the tinted windows of the captain's deck. He could make out figures moving behind them and knew they would be dressed in epaulettes and hats, but to him they were shadows resembling ghosts. It reminded him of his dream the night before. Nameless shadows. Delivering him across the waters of the Styx. He pictured himself from above, a figure between land and death, and he wondered how the fuck he had ended up here.

'What we have in the file is a summation of the case. What we can give you on request is a full transcript of the trial, but we believe that unless you have legal experience or extensive knowledge of court procedure then it is better not to bother with that. The summation is written by an independent expert and not by our department. It includes testimony and evidence given in court, but also gives clear and concise facts on how the death of Nancy Sayer occurred, who was responsible and why the death penalty was passed. Mainly that the crime was a heinous crime. You may find some of the photographs, police photographs, disturbing. It is extremely important, however, that you study everything contained in here very closely. Believe me, it will settle in your mind that Tim Hughes is without doubt guilty. That there is no possibility of an innocent man dying and that he does indeed deserve to pay the ultimate price.

'I will leave you with it now. Someone will call for you at one, possibly myself and we'll fix you with some lunch.'

The door closed. Riley ran his fingertips over the brown cover of the file. He rose and poured a cup of coffee from the machine in the corner. Mr Lewis had greeted him on arrival and whisked him straight into this room. A tiny office. One window pointing out to sea. The man appeared nervous and harassed. Constantly gazing at his watch while ushering Riley into a seat. He returned to the file, wondering if anyone was watching. If there were hidden cameras. Would they know if he didn't read it? He flipped it open and had a sense of relief. He'd half expected a gruesome picture to confront him. Instead he faced a neatly typed double-spaced page.

August 3rd started off just like any other for the Sayer family, as Nancy's mother, Kerri, describes it. 'I had trouble getting her out of bed. She wasn't lazy or anything, but like any other teenager she wasn't keen on getting up in the mornings. Especially a Saturday or Sunday. She liked to be there till lunchtime. She'd been out the night before to a party, so she looked pretty pale and worn-out when I took her up a cup of tea. That was at 10. She got dressed and ran out of the house within half an hour. She was supposed to be meeting a couple of her friends in town. I remember her turning and shouting she'd be back for tea. Usually we eat on a Saturday about 7, but I wasn't all that worried when she was late. She was a grown-up by then. Had her own key and everything. Josh, her younger brother, was in bed by 11 and I wasn't long after. Of course, I noticed in the morning that she hadn't been home, but I was annoyed more than anything. Thinking she could have phoned. As it got to late Sunday afternoon, I became more worried. I felt something was wrong. I started to think maybe she'd had an accident or got into trouble. You think the worst these days. I called her friends. Maxine said they'd gone back to hers around 3 Saturday afternoon, played some music and had a coffee. Nancy left hers at 4. According to Maxine, she was coming home. That panicked me. I called the police. They didn't seem very excited. Suggested she'd gone to her boyfriend's or something like that, but I knew that wasn't the case. She wasn't seeing anyone really and if she'd went somewhere else she'd have phoned to let me know by then. She was generally quite conscientious in that way. Of course, I didn't know, but she was already dead. I tried the rest of her friends. The hospitals. Nothing. So I called the police again. Two of them came round and took a statement and a photograph of her. They were very reassuring. Told me they were sure she'd turn up. Not to worry, they said. Teenagers run off all the time and mostly come back. I told them that Nancy wouldn't run off. Had no reason to. We were all happy together. They nodded. Said they'd be in touch.

'I remember on the Saturday when she'd popped her head round the door to say when she'd be home, she looked so young, innocent. Hardly any make-up on at all. Just a touch of a dark red lipstick I'd bought her a couple of days before. She had lovely skin, you know. I used to shout at her for covering it in so much foundation. She could easily pass for late twenties when she had all the paint on and her hair was done. I didn't stop her going out like that. Maybe that was wrong, but all girls are like that. You can't stop them growing up. But that morning she looked exactly like who she was. A beautiful young girl. And it's a funny thing, because in my heart I know that when she shouted at me I was busy. I was cleaning. I didn't turn round. I just shouted back. I didn't properly say goodbye. But in my mind I can see her. Standing by the door. Smiling.'

Nancy walked three blocks and caught a number 107 bus into the city centre. The journey takes twenty minutes. She was ten minutes late meeting her friends, as one of them, Maxine Forrestor, recalls. 'We said we'd meet her at 11, but she was a bit late, not late for Nancy though. She was always the one you were left standing waiting on. Since nobody had much money, we went window-shopping. Three of us. Me, Jane and Nancy. After an hour we got bored and had a burger and sat round chatting. Usually people pass that you know and you can have a bit of a laugh, but that day the only person we spoke to was a guy we'd known at school called Stuart Maxwell. He tried to chat us up a bit, but we told him where to go. We got back to my house about 3 and listened to some records. Then my mum and dad came in and Nancy and Jane left. About 4. Before going, Nancy asked to borrow a silver top of mine. A sparkly low-cut top. Quite tight. She changed into it before going. Jane made a joke about her having a secret date. It did seem a funny thing to put on just to go home in.'

Nancy waits with Jane at a bus stop until Jane's bus arrives. The last Jane sees of her is when they wave goodbye. As Jane says, she seems 'perfectly normal'. She is heading in the general direction of home.

It is a week later when her body is discovered. Only four miles from her home is a small stretch of woods where many locals take their dogs for exercise. This is precisely what John Donaldson was doing on Saturday 10 August. Accompanied by his two young sons, he was taking his Labrador, Jake, for his morning walk. 'It was quite chilly that morning and the two boys moaned about going out. They wanted to lie by the fire and watch TV, but I eventually got them moving. Jake was as keen as usual and bounded off ahead, but after a while he slowed and tended to stick close to us. He must have sensed what was up ahead. Dogs have a nose for these things, you know. I remember John, my youngest, throwing the ball for him and having to go and get it himself. Jake wouldn't go after it. Eventually he just wandered off the path behind us and stopped. I should say that the path we were on is quite quiet. Not many people use it, which is why I like it. You don't have to separate your dog from someone else's every five minutes. Anyway, he had stopped and was sniffing the ground. I should have had an inkling, because he was whimpering a little as well, but I was getting impatient. I shouted a few times, then went over. I bent down and grabbed his collar to pull him away and in doing so I noticed the ground was a funny colour. Bluish. Apparently it was her skin. I looked and saw that where he had been nuzzling he'd disturbed the earth and I saw her eye and her cheek. It sort of froze me. Thank God the boys were there. My next thought was to get them away. Stop them seeing anything. Otherwise I think I'd have been tearing home screaming my head off. You read about people discovering bodies, but when it happens it's unlike anything else. It kills a little piece inside yourself. I hurried the kids home and dialled 999. The police arrived and I showed them to the spot. One side of me didn't want to see much more, but the other side did. I'm not sick or anything like that. I don't hang round the scenes of accidents or chase ambulances. It's just that being the one who found her, I felt sort of responsible. That I should be there. I guessed who it was. I'd seen the papers, but she didn't look much like her picture. Her face. I guess it was the beating she took. I don't have nightmares about it, which is funny, because I thought I would. I get a bit sick of people asking me about it. It's like I'm some kind of minor celebrity in the neighbourhood. The one who found her. What I feel more than anything is guilt. Guilt that I ran away and left her lying there all the time it had taken to call the police and get them to her. I know it's stupid. That she was dead. Couldn't feel anything. But like I said, it was a chilly morning. It would have been cold in that ground. She'd been there long enough.'

Kerri positively identified Nancy from clothes and jewellery taken from the body. 'I had a little bit of hope at first when I saw the clothes, 'cause I didn't recognize the top. It had slipped my mind, but then I remembered she'd changed at Maxine's. They had the silver St Christopher I'd got her on her sixteenth birthday and her ring. A plain gold band with two little stones. Not diamond or anything, just cheap, but she really liked it and had bought it herself.'

Dental records confirmed that the body discovered in the woodland was indeed Nancy Sayer.

Forensic evidence determined that Nancy had died on the Saturday she had last been seen. Her death had been caused by strangulation. A thin line of cord was found still wound round her throat and deeply embedded into her skin. She had struggled to save her life. Suffering fractures to her cheekbones, jaw and ribs. Her left wrist was broken and several of the nails on her right hand were also broken. She had been raped.

Riley read the last sentence again. 'She had been raped.' This part of the file ended half-way down the page. He turned to the next one and found that it contained a photograph. A pleasant picture. A school photograph. The girl posed with a studied smile in front of a light blue backdrop. She wore a dark blue sweater with yellow trim. A white shirt, top button undone, and a blue and yellow striped tie. He couldn't tell if the blonde hair that flowed past her shoulders was dyed or not. Perhaps lightened a touch, since her eyebrows were a shade of light brown. She had a high forehead and large blue-grey eyes. Straight nose. Nice mouth. Nicely shaped. He imagined her natural smile came to her more easily than the strain she showed now. Her mother had been right about her skin. Barely a blemish on it. A pretty girl and Riley guessed that with a few touches of make-up a stunner. A proper heartbreaker.

'She had been raped.' He shifted uncomfortably in his seat, then started on the text below the picture.

To aid the police in their investigation Nancy's mother was asked to provide some details on the family history. What follows is in the actual words of Kerri Sayer.

'Me and David hadn't been going out long before I fell pregnant. It was sheer bad luck. We'd always used a condom. Every single time. Which, believe me, compared to my mates was pretty unusual. Of course most people think you're a slut. It's true. The world hasn't moved on that much. Even the doctor was less than understanding. David didn't really want me to have it. He didn't say as much, but I could tell he was waiting to hear the magical word abortion. There's nothing wrong with abortion. As far as I'm concerned it's every woman's right, but I just couldn't. No way. I guess that was why he didn't press me. He knew in his heart how I felt. We pretended, to other people as well as to ourselves, to be in love. I don't think we ever really were. After a couple of years the cracks appeared. David felt trapped. I felt trapped too. I love my kids, but as a mother you have even less choice. We had Josh, but it was just another desperate attempt to fool ourselves. Not long after Josh was born David left. I've hardly heard anything from him in years. He never even came to the funeral. I was a bit shocked by that. I mean, it wouldn't have been such an effort to make it to your own daughter's funeral. He sent a card, for what that's worth.

'So for most of Nancy's and practically all of Josh's life we've been a single-parent family. We've been happy though. Not a so-called dysfunctional unit. Money's tight. Always has been. David hasn't supplied us with a penny. But we've got by together and we're happy.

'Nancy's been great. She used to ask about her dad, but that eventually stopped. Now she tries to encourage me to get out and meet someone. At school she got decent marks. Not brilliant, but she was bright and could really make people laugh. There was always a lot of her friends round the house or she was punishing the phone bill. She went to college to sit some A-levels so she could go to university. She wanted to study English.

'The police asked me if she was sexually active. It makes me feel uncomfortable, that question. I know the way people think. That if she was having sex then she is more responsible for getting raped and killed than some virgin. It's not true. No one deserves to be murdered more than anyone else. It doesn't matter if she's a prostitute or a nun.

'When she was fifteen she came and told me she wanted to go on the pill. I asked her if she was sleeping with anyone. She said no. Then she told me about losing her virginity. It happened on a school holiday to France a couple of months earlier. Apparently the kids got drunk on some cheap wine and she ended up in bed with some boy she'd had a crush on for months. I could've cried. She had wanted to say no but the boy had told her that if she really loved him she'd "do it". Of course all the boy did was laugh the next day and boast to his cronies. She was really upset about it and spent weeks worrying until her period arrived. So even though she didn't have a boyfriend at the time, I let her go on the pill. Just to give her some peace of mind.

'She started to go out with Lee not long after that. He was her only steady boyfriend. They were together about eight months. I don't really know for certain if they were having sex, but I would guess that they were. He stayed at our house a couple of times but not in the same room as Nancy. I guess I'm not a modern mother in that respect. I don't know how it ended. After he stopped phoning and coming round I asked, but she said she didn't want to talk about it. I respected that. She was entitled to her privacy. From then on she went on the odd date, but as far as I know there was no one special.

'At one of the first press conferences a reporter asked me how I would describe Nancy and before I could think I answered that she was an ordinary girl. I cursed myself for that. I mean, that is what she was, but it doesn't register anything with people. It just makes her kind of faceless. She was ordinary, but like any ordinary person there were extraordinary things about her. Special things. Nobody laughed the way Nancy did. Nobody understood me like Nancy. She always saw if I was upset or down no matter how hard I tried to hide it. She knew and she'd give me a big hug.

'She loved to have her feet rubbed. Some nights in front of the telly I'd spend hours doing what Nancy liked to call "my duty". You had to be careful though, she hated it if you put your finger between her toes. She'd jump. Almost hit the ceiling. Now and again, if she was being cheeky, I'd do it deliberately. She'd start off shouting but we always ended up laughing. I know it doesn't sound like much but it's these sorts of things I want to tell about Nancy. I want to somehow get it across who she was. Someone who didn't deserve to die.'

The first theory from the police working on the case was that Nancy had been abducted. Lured into a car or van by someone, possibly someone she knew, then driven to the spot in the woods and killed. Perhaps a sexual assault that had gone too far. However, there was an anomaly in the forensic evidence. The bruising and tears in and around her anus were consistent with a violent rape, but there was a distinct lack of bruising in or around her vagina. This suggested she may have had consensual sex. Of course, after being raped the first time she may not have been able to struggle in the second instance, but there was also the possibility that vaginal sex had been first and consensual. Likely to be with someone she knew very well.

The first puzzle the police concentrated on was how she got to the woods. Although the spot was only four miles from her home, it was seven miles from where Jane Summerton had waved goodbye to her. A fair distance to walk. It seemed safe to assume she hadn't done so. Nor is the wood on a recognizable bus route. The nearest route passing in line with where Nancy was last seen was canvassed. No driver on the route that Saturday recalled seeing her or any girl of a similar description. Therefore it seemed plausible she had gone there by car. Either against her will or with someone she knew and would agree to take a lift from.

The first suspect the police had to check, of course, was the last male known to have had contact with her. The boy in the burger bar. Stuart Maxwell. Mr Maxwell could account for his movements for the remainder of that Saturday through testimony of his friends and family. However, he did put a slightly different slant on the conversation that had taken place between him and the girls.

'I'd been in there with a couple of mates. They'd gone off to watch football. I didn't go. I hate football. Anyway, I was on my way out when Nancy said, "Hello." It kinda made me laugh, since I knew what they were after. I hadn't known any of them at school but I'd see them at college and about at clubs and I'd pass on a bit of dope to them now and then. I'm not a dealer or anything, it's just that if you have some and you're at a party then people ask. Before you know it, when you bump into them in the street they're asking. I never made any money out of it, I just got back what I paid. The last time I'd given them some I'd been pretty smashed and they'd said they'd pay me later. They were skint. I didn't mind at the time, being pretty out of it. Needless to say I never saw any money. So eventually they got round to, "Have you got any?" Being a bit flash and wanting to rub it in, I pulled this large chunk of dope out of my pocket and casually said, "Just this." Of course, their eyes popped and it was, "Give us some", so I said, "Sure, if you pay up, including for last time." That's when they laid out the same line about being broke and settling with me later. I just laughed. Said no chance. I guess I was feeling spiteful. Really wanting to piss them off. Otherwise I would never have said it, but I said kinda jokingly, "You could always suck my cock for some." I know it's a horrible thing to say, but I said it jokingly. Without really thinking. Nancy went nuts. Calling me a dirty so and so. An AIDS carrier. She looked really mean. Full of hate. The other two were telling her to calm down. I suppose they were still thinking of the dope. The one, Jane, kept saying, "He was only joking", but she wouldn't let up. "Your cock's full of AIDS." She must have said that half a dozen times, even after I apologized. I know it was a crap thing to say, but I was still taken aback at her reaction. I'd never seen her like that. She always seemed quite easygoing. Always laughing. I mean, I'd always been good to them.

Just 'cause you've got dope doesn't mean you have to give it to anyone who asks. It's not a moral obligation. I felt quite hurt afterwards. Considering all I'd done for them.'

Nancy's former boyfriend, Lee Richardson, was also questioned. He too could account for his movements that weekend. Lee was asked when he had last seen Nancy. 'I saw her at a party a couple of weeks before she disappeared. I didn't really speak to her. It's been awkward since we split.' Lee was then asked why the relationship had finished.

'It was my fault. I started to catch her out. Just odd little things. She'd tell me she'd been somewhere when I knew she hadn't. Saying she was staying at home on certain nights and I'd phone and she was out. I got it into my head she was seeing someone else. Lying to me. She just denied it. Then she came out with the "You don't own me" spiel. We had a massive argument one night and that was it. Over. I guess I was being stupid, because after that she never went out with anyone else. There obviously wasn't anyone waiting in the wings. It had all been in my head.'

The first clues to Nancy's fate came after a two-week campaign in newspapers and on television by the police and by Nancy's family. A certain Mrs Edwards called the police to report she had seen Nancy on the day of her disappearance.

'I only noticed her because she was in a car with our neighbour, Mr Hughes. I was on my way back from the shops when I saw them. They were waiting at lights on Highgate Road. I waved a hello at Mr Hughes. That's when I noticed the girl. I know he doesn't have kids, so I assumed it was one of his pupils. Him being a teacher.'

This in fact proved to be the case. Mr Hughes did indeed teach Nancy English for two years before she left for college.

The first interview with Mr Hughes took place at his home and was conducted by two officers. He appeared calm and composed. One officer asked Mr Hughes if there was any occasion on which Nancy Sayer had been in his car. Mr Hughes replied without hesitation, 'Yes. I gave her a lift a while ago. I was driving down to the shops to get a paper when I passed her. I stopped. We had a quick chat. You know, "How are you getting along?" sort of thing. Then she asked for a ride to the shops. So I dropped her there.'

The officer then asked Mr Hughes when this was. Mr Hughes claimed the incident took place well over a month ago. The officer then asked if it couldn't have been more recent. Mr Hughes stated that he didn't think so, since he had been practically housebound for weeks because of a virus. However, he agreed it was possible, since time had become confused for him because of his illness. His illness was confirmed by his GP, his wife and the school where he worked. Mr Hughes was then asked, in the light of Nancy's death, why he hadn't reported this incident to the police. Mr Hughes replied that since it had taken place a long time ago he didn't think it was relevant information. Mr Hughes was then confronted with the fact that a witness had sighted Nancy in his car on the day of her disappearance. At this Mr Hughes appeared dumbfounded and in a state of shock. 'They must have got their date wrong. It was before that.' Mr Hughes eventually agreed that perhaps he had given her a ride on that day but hadn't realized the significance of the date due to illness. Mr Hughes was then asked in which direction Nancy had walked when he left her. Mr Hughes stated that he didn't know, since he had simply said goodbye and then gone into the newsagent's without looking.

There were several questions raised by the evidence the police had so far. For instance, where Nancy had been going when she accepted the lift from Tim Hughes, since to the shops from Highgate Road almost doubles back to where she had come from, the bus stop where Jane Summerton had last seen her. Perhaps Mrs Edwards had the date wrong, but she was certain of the date because it coincided with her husband's birthday. It followed logically that Nancy had already been to her destination. A check with family and friends failed to bring to light anyone she could have been visiting in that area. Then there was the change of clothes and the suspicions of her boyfriend Lee. Had Nancy gone for a secret rendezvous, then on her way home been abducted? Or perhaps the person she went to meet was the killer.

The autopsy revealed that Nancy had alcohol in her system. Maxine Forrestor, in a later interview, admitted the three girls had been drinking. 'When we got back to the house I opened a bottle of Bacardi my mum had. My parents always have a few bottles in the house. They never know how much is in them. But it was only a couple of Bacardi and Cokes. That was all we had.' The police determined that the amount of alcohol in Nancy's system constituted more than a couple of Bacardi and Cokes. Where else had she been drinking? The check with Tim Hughes's school revealed that he had reported sick on the Monday following Nancy's disappearance. His wife told police that he had been taken ill on the Saturday night, called the doctor on the Sunday and still hadn't fully recovered. No further connection between Hughes and Nancy could be made. Nor was there anything in Tim Hughes's background to suggest that he was the culprit. That was until detectives leading the inquiry received a phone call from a Mr John Williams.

One side of the wood where Nancy was found borders a large park. There is also a square of tarmac where people regularly leave their cars when visiting the park. This area had been canvassed daily by police but nobody could recall seeing Nancy in a vehicle on that Saturday.

Mr Williams had returned from his annual vacation at his timeshare villa in Spain. 'I couldn't believe it when I read the papers. It was only a small item by then but I recognized her immediately. It stuck in my mind because of the date. The day before we flew. I'd gone into town to get a few last-minute things and I'd taken my grandson with me. I'd been promising the little fella a kick-about with his ball all day, so I stopped on the way home at the park. No sooner had I parked than two people jumped up in the car next to me. The girl was nearer to me and seemed pretty embarrassed. She was fussing with her hair and pretending I wasn't there. I avoided looking at them proper. Figuring it was a young couple at it, so to speak. They got out of the car and walked into the woods. That's when I noticed the man was a lot older than her. He had long grey hair. I did wonder if she was a prostitute, what with them being in the car and the age difference. I can't remember the make of the car but it was a large car and light blue. It was still there when we left, after maybe twenty minutes. As I said, I avoided a proper look, but I saw enough and it was definitely Nancy.'

Tim Hughes has long grey hair and drives a large blue car. He was taken into custody on 24 August. At first Mr Hughes denied driving Nancy to the woods, but later changed his story when told of the evidence of John Williams.

'Like I said before, I passed her in the car and she waved me down. She asked where I was going and I told her to the newsagent's. I had felt this fever coming on since morning and there was no paracetamol in the house, so I popped out for some. She asked for a lift to the woods. Said she was late meeting a friend there.'

'Did she say who?'

'No, just a friend. I agreed, since it wasn't far out of my way. We chatted in the car about exams and about her applying for university. She thought she was doing well. We got there and she got out and I drove home.'

'Not to the newsagent's?'

'Obviously I stopped off there.'

'Did Nancy appear drunk?'

'No.'

'So she got out and walked into the woods alone and you drove home?'

'Yes. I mean no. Come to think of it, I got out as well and walked with her a little way. I thought the air might make me feel better. I remember asking her where she was meeting her friend and she seemed quite vague about it. I think she said, "Around here", and I wondered if she was actually meeting anyone at all.'

At this point in the interview there occurred a pause while officers arranged for coffee to be served, during which Mr Hughes made the following statement. 'I know this looks suspicious, I know I lied before, but you have to believe me that Nancy was fine when I left her. I never touched her.'

'Why did you lie, Tim?'

'I only realized the date I'd given her the lift when the police came round. I got scared. Simple as that. I knew how it would look.'

'Well, you have to see it from our point of view, Tim, it does look pretty bad. Why would Nancy ask for a lift if she wasn't meeting anyone?'

'I don't know. Perhaps she was bored and just killing time.'

'Maybe. You don't have to worry, Tim. We'll do a few tests and then I'm sure we'll know the truth.'

'What sort of tests?'

An overwhelming amount of forensic evidence quickly accumulated against Tim Hughes. Semen samples were positively matched. Skin traces taken from underneath the broken nails of Nancy's right hand, where she had tried to fight off her attacker, were also matched.

A turn of page revealed a photograph. A hand resting palm upwards on a bed of soil. Fingers curled. The edges of the clear-varnished nails sharply focused and shining jaggedly like a snow-capped mountain range in an aerial picture. The skin had a translucent quality. A blue and greyish tone except for on the forearm, where there was an ugly purplish, veiny bruise. At the base of the thumb a cut. Very straight. Very deep.

Below the photograph a statement in brackets:

(NOTE CUT WHERE SPADE STRUCK AND PIERCED SKIN.)

Riley shuddered. He heard the sound of the spade striking. The crunch of the boot following on. Driving the spade deep into the earth through the edge of her hand.

The following page contained only a short paragraph and he let his eyes settle a moment on the calming white of the paper before reading.

A spade found by officers in Mr Hughes's garden shed revealed soil on a par with the soil of the woods. A different alkalinity from the soil in Mr Hughes' garden. The spade also held small traces of blood. Nancy's blood. A jacket of Mr Hughes contained matching hair and blood samples. Cord, of the type used to strangle Nancy Sayer, was discovered tied around Mr Hughes's roses.

Riley knew there would be a photograph on the next page. One eye was closed. Battered. The eyelid thick, puffy, like the cheek below it. The other eye open. This surprised him. He hadn't known before that dead people's eyes could be open. She had been laid out for this portrait on a black background. The cord she had been killed with curled and twisted across the picture. Stained red, black and brown like a piece of wire on a fence post. Exposed to the wind and rain for years. The colour of blood was also a revelation to him. The variety of colour. Light transparent traces that ran under her eyes in a stripe. Bright rich flecks on her forehead that shone as if still moist. The dark solid mass that flowed out from her nostrils, caked her upper lip and her jaw. Coated her hair. There was no horror. Instead, perhaps due to the lighting the photographer had used, Riley felt a glow emanated from Nancy's face. He felt tender towards the picture. That as if by touching the surface he could in some way reach her because she was still there. He could see her behind the one eye that was still open. Frozen in the pain of the moment.

He considered flicking back to the school picture to compare, but discarded the idea. That Nancy was gone. This was Nancy. This was who she had become.

Riley turned to the final page.

Tim Hughes gave one last version of events that, despite the forensic evidence to the contrary, he stuck by throughout the trial. This is what he said.

'I took her to the woods. She couldn't keep quiet. She chattered the whole way at a hundred miles an hour. She seemed excited. I could tell she'd been drinking. It didn't take me long to realize she was flirting with me. The way she kept leaning into me. Showing off her cleavage. I wasn't sure at first, but I wasn't imagining it, and I have to admit I felt flattered. She was a beautiful girl and had left school. That's important to remember, she was of age. There wasn't anything ethically wrong with it. When we got there my fever was running high and I felt lousy. She touched my forehead and made a comment about how I could do with some looking after. She stroked my forehead and we kissed a couple of times. She initiated the kissing, not me. I got out my hip flask and we both had a few pulls on it. I thought we needed to calm down. It was happening so bloody fast. One minute I was popping to the shops, the next this. She started prattling on about how friends need friends, and I guess I was in a sort of shock, because I didn't realize what she was getting at until she mentioned about being skint at college and how she could do with some looking after as well. At this point she put her hand on my thigh and slid it along to my crotch. She squeezed a little and asked if I knew what she meant. I didn't react. She must have taken this for a yes. She was so confident. Not the slightest trace of nerves. She told me later she'd done it before. Anyway, she said twenty pounds would see her all right. I must have nodded or something, I don't recall, but she undid my trousers then. She'd only just started when a car pulled in alongside us. We both panicked and tried to sort ourselves out. After a minute we calmed down and she suggested a walk in the woods. We had sex there. I offered her thirty but she said no, that we'd agreed on twenty. I left her in the woods. She was alive and well. There was no violence involved.'

As the prosecuting counsel stated at the trial, Mr Hughes's testimony could not account for how his semen was found in Nancy's rectum nor his skin beneath her broken fingernails. The jury took twenty minutes to find Tim Hughes guilty and recommend death. On the evidence available, there could have been no other just outcome to this case.

Riley closed the file. The final line stayed with him: 'there could have been no other just outcome'. It was indisputable. Did this man deserve to die? Was he saying that? He'd voted for it. Nancy Sayer didn't deserve it.

The door opened and Mr Lewis smiled at him. 'I'm so sorry, Mr Scott. You must be starving.'

'Eh?'

'It's way past 1. I've just been inundated. Come and I'll get you some lunch.'

Riley followed him out of the door. The man took hold of his arm gently.

'I feel it is my duty to let you know. Word came through on the appeal. Rejected. It's all systems go.'

The Machine

The food had no taste and Riley could not recall consuming it. His movements were automatic, as were his responses to Lewis's conversation. He couldn't summon any panic or fear. He wondered if the dishwater he'd been served as coffee was laced with Valium. If so he was glad, for at this moment in time any sense of detachment had to be welcomed, because he knew that eventually the reality of his situation would sink in.

'I'm sorry about the quality of the lunch.'

'That's OK. It was fine really.' Riley wanted to alleviate the look of distress on the man's face. 'Perfectly edible, which is the main thing.' He pushed the plate away from himself.

'Edible but stinking.' Lewis stacked the plates on top of each other and put them on a tray. 'We're lucky to have plates. The staff canteen is out of action just now, so everyone's on the POW's grub.'

'POW?'

'Yeah. Prisoner of war. I'm afraid it's very much us against them in here. The food used to be better, but we had to downgrade it after bad press. Too many headlines about serving up hotel treatment. You piss off either the inmates or the public, you can't win. I usually bring an apple and a sandwich myself.'

69

'So it's my fault you had to suffer.'

Lewis laughed. The kind of laugh that annoyed Riley. No mouth to it. All the action in the nose, as if he was having trouble clearing his sinuses.

'I guess it is your fault.'

'You know, I thought we might meet the other candidates today.'

'I see. No, we keep you apart. Anonymity is guaranteed. Any unforeseen encounter in the future could prove awkward for either parties involved.'

Lewis checked his watch. He pushed the tray aside and his chair back in one motion. 'We better be getting along. You've got to be with our Mr Johnson.'

'Who's Mr Johnson?'

'He's a man with a certain expertise in dealing with cases like Mr Hughes.'

Riley looked confused. He knew what Lewis meant but wanted him to say it.

Lewis fiddled with his coffee cup before elaborating. 'He's the hangman.'

'But I thought you were the hangman.'

Lewis laughed again. Riley winced. 'Good God, no. An executioner needs strength and personality. I'm just a faceless penpusher.'

On the way they passed a prison guard. Tall and broad-shouldered. Black overalls. A short wooden stick and shining handcuffs dangling from a black leather belt. Keys tinkling off his thigh in time with his stride.

Lewis broke into a grin. 'How's things, Simon?'

The guard grinned back. 'If all goes according to plan, we'll be hosing shit off the walls on Sunday again.'

'Not me. I'll be at home with my slippers on.'

'You're a lucky man.'

The thump of the guard's boots echoed off the walls and

ceiling of the white metal corridor.

Lewis whispered out of the side of his mouth, 'Between you and me, he makes a papal decree seem forgiving, but he does keep order in here.'

'What did he mean about shit?'

'There's usually a lot of excitement and a few other things in the air when there's an execution.'

They went through a white steel door into another white corridor, only now it had a blue stripe running along one wall.

'Why the stripe?' Riley asked.

'It means there's no POW's in this area. Ah, here we are.' They stopped at an elevator. 'We have to go down a few floors.'

Riley noticed a Gents' sign. 'Can I use the loo?'

'Sure. Go ahead. I'll wait here.'

The cold water brought a tingle to his skin, which he examined in the mirror above the basin. The fluorescent lights did nothing to flatter him. Every blemish, every pore being harshly illuminated. He rubbed at a small black hole on the bridge of his nose. It remained where it was. A reminder of a huge spot prematurely burst in his teenage years. He squeezed two whiteheads near his Adam's apple and just visible through the stubble he had acquired in the past couple of days. It stung like hell. The pain and another quick rinse with cold water made him feel as though he was emerging from his deep sleep.

Beside the exit door, mounted on the wall, was a phone. Riley lifted the receiver. Nothing. Instructions told him to press nine for an outside line. He did so and was rewarded with a dialling tone.

'Holden and Bernard.'

'Susan, is he in?'

'Sorry, who is calling please?'

'Riley.'

'Who?'

Perhaps it wasn't her. She could be sick or having the day off. It could be a temp. But it sounded like her. The voice broke into his thoughts.

'Is that Riley the breaker of promises? The man who shows no sensitivity for others' feelings and needs.'

'Oh, fuck.' He'd forgotten the chocolate débâcle. 'You're not still going on about chocolates?'

'Did I mention chocolates? I don't think I did. It seems to me that it's your guilty conscience that brought chocolates to mind. In answer to your question, no, he is not in.'

'Please, Susan, don't do this. I'll buy you two boxes.'

'He still isn't in.'

'Three boxes.'

'Really, he isn't in.'

'I'll buy you the biggest, most expensive box of chocolates in the history of chocolate-making. Just put me through.'

'That's great, Riley, but absolutely, upon my soul, Andrew isn't in his office.'

'Oh.'

'Yes. It may come as a surprise to you, but even though I am female I cannot jeopardize relations with clients of the firm on personal whims. I may have breasts, I may have periods, but it's no excuse in front of an industrial tribunal.'

'OK. I know. I'm feeling a bit stressed. Do you know where he is? Did he leave any message for me?'

'He's meeting some luminary of the bar and no, there isn't any message. He'll be back around 4.'

'Can you tell him to call me after 5 please?'

'Politeness gets you everywhere. How big is my chocolate box now?'

'Obscenely large.'

'Then I shall do so.'

★

Riley and Lewis focused on the numbers indicating the floors they dropped by as the elevator descended. Riley cleared his throat noisily to break the silence and as a prelude to a question.

'Have you read the file on Hughes?'

'Yes, I have.'

'There's a couple of things I don't quite understand.'

'I don't really know any more about the case than you do. All I've read is the file and what's in the papers.'

'It's him saying Nancy was a prostitute. I don't understand that. He must have known he wouldn't be believed. That he would be convicted.'

'Who knows what people who commit these crimes think.'

'But why say it? And worse, never retract it. It must have hurt her family.'

Lewis scrutinized the floor numbers more intently. 'Yes, I believe it did cause distress. Especially to the mother.'

'So why say it?'

'Perhaps it was his intention to cause distress. I don't know though. That's just speculation.'

'Have you met him?'

'A couple of times. Briefly.'

'What is he like?'

'He doesn't say much does Mr Hughes. Anyway –' Lewis smiled at Riley – 'you'll get to meet him yourself, eventually.'

The man didn't rise from his seated position. He shook Riley's hand firmly and indicated with a glance where he should sit. He spoke in a whispery tone, as if worried that they were going to be overheard by an eavesdropper.

'My name's Johnson. We'll stick to surnames, as I don't really think we're in what you would call an informal situation. I'm a staunch family man. I've got a wife and two sons. The eldest graduated from university this year. That's something I'm pretty proud of, even though it cost me a fortune. I've got a mortgage and a bit of garden I like to grow things in. Vegetables mainly. My potatoes have long been a source of amusement to my family. They never grow bigger than a golf ball. It doesn't matter what I do, they're more like peas than potatoes. If I'm lucky I manage a couple of weeks in the sun a couple of times a year. I did miss something vital in this résumé. I hang people. I'm the state executioner.

'You're here to help me. I don't want your life story. I want your cooperation. I simply tell you all this so you can understand that I am the same as you, an ordinary guy. There's nothing strange or exceptional about me. I'm telling you this so you can understand why you're here.

'We have a job to do. That's all that concerns me, the job. I'm well aware that the convictions you held when you put your cross in the yes box may not be as strong now. You may even have changed your mind completely now that you're here. Now that the death penalty is suddenly a reality. But you have to forget that. You see, you are not the most important person involved in this situation.' Johnson stabbed his own chest with a thick blunt forefinger. 'I am not the most important person either. It's Tim Hughes we have to think of now. He's our focus. From the second I step into that cell, everything has to be done in a precise and efficient manner. Speed is crucial. Although we can't rush around as if in a panic. Panic is infectious. We have to be controlled. The machinery has to run smoothly and you, Mr Scott, are only a part of that machinery.' Mr Johnson's grey eyes with golden flecks streaked across them misted over as if all emotion had evaporated and he was studying the said machine in a haze of logic. 'We are not, in essence, killing a man. Society has already carried out that task. We are the mechanics carrying out the job. A job of precision. It's a far more sophisticated process than in the past, when a length of rope was slung over the branch of a tree and some poor bugger strangled to death.' Johnson's eyes narrowed as he visualized the scene more clearly. 'When I enter the cell, there will be you, the governor of the prison and two guards. I'll place the waist strap around the prisoner, which pins his arms to his side. The governor reads out his conviction and sentence. We leave the holding room. Four guards in the corridor. We two walk at the rear. It's a short distance to the room containing the gallows. No more than a few steps. Unless the prisoner resists, and it's unlikely he will, it's up to you and me once we're in there.'

'But what if he does resist, go mad?'

'The guards will restrain him. With his arms pinned to his side, there isn't much he can do. They would also carry him on to the gallows in such an event. We would do nothing until he is on the gallows. You generally find that men in the position of Hughes have in fact resigned themselves to their fate. They know they cannot escape. Believe it or not, history shows that most men walk on their own to their death. So, if all goes well, we take over. Lead him up the steps. You will be required to do the minimal. Hopefully that will decrease the likelihood of disruption or mishap.' Mr Johnson stroked his chin. Tracing back to the position he had left the prisoner in. 'We'll go into more details during our rehearsals tomorrow. Positioning is of prime importance. We don't want to be bumping into each other and looking like fools. All I'll go through just now is the running order. It's very simple. I'll attach the leg straps to keep his feet together. You place the hood over his head. I'll apply the noose. You take out the safety pin on the lever. I readjust the noose, making sure it's placed properly and securely. I step back. I will nod. You wait for the signal, the nod, then pull the lever.' Mr Johnson's hand scythed through the air and banged on to the table he sat on. He smiled at Riley. 'It sounds a lot, but with a bit of practice I'm sure we can get it down to ten to fifteen seconds. The closer to ten the better.'

Riley's chest tightened. He took a deep breath and looked round the room. The rows of desks behind him. The blackboard facing with smudges of chalk. Dusted particles of old lessons. Except for the lack of windows, just another classroom. Similar to the one he himself had been taught in.

'I can see this disturbs you, Mr Scott, and that's understandable, but once you've got into the mechanics of this type of thing, the shock tends to wear off.' Mr Johnson patted him on the shoulder. 'You'll be fine.'

'That's if it is me and not one of the others.'

For a second Riley searched for a sign from the lined and craggy face of Mr Johnson, but Mr Johnson just nodded and lifted his bulky frame off the corner of the desk he had been perched on. He shuffled across to a cupboard near the blackboard, rubbing one buttock. A shorter man than Riley had first thought. Not much over five feet, but with a chest as wide. A gut that balanced precariously on the edge of his belt as if waiting for a little more time to take the plunge. His arms appeared to have been cut off from someone much larger and stuck to him. Riley realized the illusion was due to the way he walked. In a crouch. Knees bent. Shoulders slightly hunched. However, this didn't account for the hands. These too seemed out of proportion. Riley tried to tell himself that he was being foolish and putting a significance on them that wasn't there because of the work these hands carried out. That they were just workmen's hands. The rough skin he had felt when shaking them. The dirty broken fingernails and the scars he had noticed a record of years of being put to practical use. But Riley couldn't escape the chill and fear that had emanated from the hands upon contact and spread into his body. They were brutal on the eyes. The skin, although rough, was pale. A sickly washed-out pink. It reminded him of cheap chicken roll in a supermarket deli. Meat fashioned from pieces recovered from factory machines and discarded flesh that no one else, in its original form, had wanted but now served a purpose for the poor. The fingers and the back of the hands sprouted a matt of curly white hair without shine. Lank and lifeless. Starved of nutrition and light. Nothing for the roots of those hairs to feed on from the blue veins that coursed beneath the skin.

From the cupboard Johnson took out a black leather bag and put it on the desk he had been sitting on.

'I'll show you some of the equipment and you can get a feel of it before tomorrow. This is the leg strap.' A curled-up length of thick brown leather with a square metal buckle landed on the desk. 'Waist strap.' Similar but much wider and with a leather cuff attached to each side.

Riley fingered the soft, smooth surface of the worn leather and the rough underside. 'These seem really old.'

'They are. They were in use before hanging was first abolished in 1964. In fact they were worn by Peter Anthony Allen, the last man hanged in Britain until our recent resumption. Hood.'

The soft white material landed on the back of Riley's hands. He held it in front of his face. A simple cotton bag.

'Why white? I always thought the hoods were black.'

'That's the movies. They've always been white. It's tradition. I don't know why though. Maybe it's to make a point about the purity of justice.' He laughed.

'I can't believe how relaxed you are.'

'I don't have anything to worry about. Neither should you. If you are worrying, you have some serious questions to ask yourself about choices you've made in life.'

'I just never expected to be here.'

'Neither did I. You shouldn't feel too sorry for yourself. You're not in that unusual a situation. Other countries have citizens witnessing the death penalty process. America, for example.'

'Yeah, but I'm not just a witness.'

'No. That's true. Think of it this way, would you rather be in your position or on the end of a rope?'

'It's not much of a choice.'

'That's where you're wrong. There was a choice and you made it, as did Mr Hughes. You don't know much about hanging, do you, Mr Scott?'

'No.'

'Most people don't. I don't think they even bothered to find out during the referendum. They just like the simplicity of the idea. An eye for an eye and we'll all be safer in the world. As long as it's a press report and not real flesh and blood. I guess it's easier for them that way. It's silly though. There's nothing to be frightened of. The truth is never anything to be frightened of. Hanging's an ancient form of execution. Probably the most popular choice in the world. We have a great history of it in this country. We perfected it. For example, during the reign of Henry VIII, seventy-two thousand men were executed. However, since it's such a cheap and easy way of killing a man, it became a much-abused system. Practically any landowner in the country could string you up in the old days. It's controlled now. We don't sell parts of the rope as souvenirs these days. As for Hughes, unlike those seventy-two thousand, he won't choke to death. That's what hanging used to be, a crushing of the jugular vein and the carotid arteries. Not any different from me doing the job with my hands, except it took longer. A good five minutes if you were lucky. In that era they even let friends of the condemned pull on their legs to try and help them on their way. Think of that being your job.' Johnson smiled reassuringly at Riley's worried frown. 'Don't worry, there's no chance of that nowadays. A man called Marwood in the 1870s brought back an idea from the previous century, the drop. An idea polished to perfection by an executioner named Berry. He calculated that a man had to fall a distance, comparative to his weight, so that the striking force at termination would be 2,680 pounds. Doesn't mean much to you, but it's a vital piece of information. Too little force and our friend Hughes will dangle on the end of the rope like a fish trying to return to the sea. Too much and we're in for a shower of blood and a scramble round the room to try and locate the head.' Riley flinched. 'My language may be a bit base for your taste, Mr Scott, but what I'm trying to impress on you is that we have a method, developed over a long period of time, and it's the best method possible. When Tim Hughes falls through that trap door, he's carrying hundreds of years of experience with him. Experience that means he'll suffer as little as possible and die as humanely as possible. His spinal column snaps. This causes complete loss of sensation. In other words, he doesn't feel a thing. He is unconscious. His breathing stops in seconds. Our job is to get the method down pat. To help Hughes we forget about Hughes. We concentrate on the job. The machine. OK?'

'OK.' Riley spoke quietly, so as not to smother the words inside his head: 'Please, God, get me out of this.'

'If you get to your feet, I'll show you how everything sets up.'

'What do you mean?'

'Stand up and I'll show you how all the gear goes on.'

'What? On me?'

'That's right.'

Riley shook his head to say no. Despite his protest, Johnson lifted him from under the arms until he had to stand to prevent the both of them crashing to the floor.

'That's it, up we go. You need to get a feel for the equipment as soon as possible.'

'Listen, I don't think I want to do this.'

'Don't be silly.' Johnson took the waist strap and put it around Riley. 'This isn't uncomfortable. It's like wearing one of those band things that men wear with tuxedos. What are they called?'

'Cummerbunds.'

'That's right. Just like them. You're quite thin, aren't you? You're almost at the last notch. It's usually only women I use that hole on.'

Riley felt as if his insides were being squashed in a vice.

'It has to be tight to avoid any movement. There's only one breakage we want.' He took Riley's arms and placed them in the cuffs, pinning them to his sides. 'Of course, Hughes will be in handcuffs, but this is as effective even without them. Right. Try and get out of that.' Johnson took a step back to give him space.

Riley strained and twisted but couldn't shift his hands. Johnson had to push him upright twice as he lost balance through his contortions. By the time he conceded defeat, he was out of breath, sweating and his shoulders were aching.

'See, nothing you can do.'

Riley didn't appreciate the triumphant, cheerful tone in the man's voice.

'Now for the legs.'

'Fine. It's done.' He was getting irritated. 'I get the idea.'

'It'll only take a second.' Before Riley could protest any further, Johnson was on his knees and the strap was in place above his ankles. Johnson rose in front of Riley with a beaming smile. 'There you go.' He raised his eyebrows in delight. 'Or should I say, there you don't go.' He laughed at his own joke. The laugh stopped suddenly. 'Just the hood.'

'Look, that's fine. I told you, I get it.'

Johnson turned his back on Riley, ignoring him.

'Mr Johnson, do you hear me? I don't want you to.'

Johnson whipped round. Riley tried to duck away from him, but the white cloth came over his head. A hand rested on his shoulder. A voice spoke to him in a hushed whisper in his left ear.

'Careful, sonny. You'll injure yourself. There isn't any noose to hold you.'

'Fuck, man, let me out of this. Let me out.' His eyes couldn't penetrate the cloth that seemed to fill his nostrils and his mouth with every breath. He jerked his head up and down violently in the hope of shifting the hood but failed. 'Do you hear me, Mr Johnson? Johnson? Do you hear me? Let me out. Let me out, man.'

No response to his shouting. He listened for a second, forcing himself to be quiet. He could hear nothing. No sign of anyone being close to him. No breathing. No footsteps. He couldn't even make out the ticking of the clock that he knew was on a wall in the room. He could hear only the thump of his own heart and the blood that it pumped rushing through his veins. His bladder reacted and he had to tighten his muscles to stop himself from peeing. His body trembled then started to shake.

'Fuck. Fuck. Johnson? What's going on? Are you there?' He tried to twist his hands free from the cuffs, even though he knew it was futile. Something else went over his head. 'Johnson.' Whatever it was gripped his throat. Crushed his Adam's apple into his windpipe. He wanted to swallow. Couldn't. His breath barely made it down into his lungs. He was jerked up on to his toes by a force behind his left ear. 'What the fuck?' The words stuck in his throat, echoed in his brain. What the fuck is going on? He tried to pull his head away, but the pressure round his throat only got worse. 'What the fuck? A noose.' The thought hit him like a train entering a tunnel. All his senses started to crowd in on him. The cloth wrapped round his head, smothering him. The rope forcing his bottom teeth through his skull. The leather cuffs biting into his skin. A noose. I'm going to hang. They're hanging me. Why?

The voice returned by his ear. 'We place the knot behind your left ear.'

Riley couldn't picture Johnson's face. Instead he saw the grey shadows of his nightmare. They had brought him here and now they were going to kill him.

'When you drop, the knot rotates a quarter clockwise.'

The rope turned. Its movement searing his skin. Shutting off his last meagre supply of air.

'It ends beneath your jaw. Like this.'

A sudden tug. His jaw thrust into the air. His teeth ground together. Cracking. Splintering. His tongue swelling, sealing off the final filter of air.

'This action means the spinal column snaps at the third vertebra.'

A finger jabbed sharply into the nape of his neck. His nerves shot back into life and out of their tunnel in a roar that tore past his lips. He threw his body forward as best he could. He was falling. Waiting for the snap that would separate him from the world. Arms pinned his chest and his descent was slowed as if he was sinking in water.

Light burst harshly into his eyes. Then came darkness. The darkness eventually formed itself into the features of Mr Johnson, who stared at him in an expressionless manner.

'You're all right. You're safe. Take a few deep breaths.'

Riley did as he was told.

'Sweet as honey, isn't it?'

'Yeah.'

'Yeah.' Johnson smiled gently. 'Now you know. It doesn't get any worse than that.'

'No.'

'No. I had to show you.' Mr Johnson sounded apologetic. 'We don't want to do that to Tim Hughes.'

'No.'

'Do you know how long you stood with that hood on before you panicked?'

'How long?'

'Twenty-five seconds. Doesn't sound long but I bet it felt long enough.'

'It did.'

Johnson softly stroked Riley's cheek. His eyes filled with a deep sadness. 'That's why the machine has to work. Ten to fifteen seconds and there isn't any panic. There isn't any distress. It'll all have gone off before he even realizes it's happening. The machine has to work. We'll make the machine work. Won't we?'

'Yeah.'

Johnson continued to stroke Riley's cheek. 'Yes. Of course we will.'

Rain lashed against the car. Wind buffeted them from side to side.

'I'm afraid it'll take us a while to get you home.'

Riley stared at the back of the driver's head. A different driver from the one he had had previously. Young with blond hair and a more chatty disposition.

'This road's a hellhole in the rush hour. Although it's not too bad at the moment. Could be worse.'

Riley felt his eyelids drooping as the heating in the car took effect.

'I've seen myself lucky to get five yards in half an hour some days. So much for the new public transport scheme to get us all out of cars.'

The driver continued to speak but his words faded and Riley drifted away. The heat in the car intensified until he thought he could detect a burning smell in the air. His cheeks were glowing. A blanket descended, covering him entirely. With his eyes closed, he reached for the switch on the door to lower the window. Taste fresh air and the rain. Before he could do so a large sickly pale hand loomed into his vision. Gripping him. Fingers pressing his eyeballs into their sockets. His eyes snapped open. Rain still splattered on the window. The driver still prattled on. The car still crawled along the motorway. They seemed to have moved no further on.

★

83

For a long time he stayed by the window of his flat without any light. Simply watching the people passing below and contemplating the message left by Andrew. His friend had sounded chirpy but Riley hadn't found the news comforting.

'Hello, Riley, it's your lawyer here. It's just after 5 and I'm pretty bushed. I've spent most of today and yesterday lobbying on your behalf. Exemption through the official channels is pretty much impossible. Don't get yourself into a panic, though, 'cause I'm sure that with a bit of encouragement behind the scenes we'll be able to sort something out. We'll have to. After all, we can't do without your silky midfield skills on Saturday. We'll get trounced. I won't be home tonight. I'm working on a chum who might give us some leeway.

'The other hopeful piece of information is that apparently Hughes came extremely close on the appeal and this is being brought to the attention of the Home Secretary, who, so word says, will give in and commute the sentence. Although he's not going to do that tonight or tomorrow. He'll leave it close, let Hughes sweat it out and prove to the press that he isn't a big softie. So the chances are he won't announce it until Saturday night. Of course, we'll have some insurance anyway.

'OK, I've got to go. There's a steak on a plate with my name on it. Give me a ring tomorrow morning at the office, and I know it's easy to say, but try not to be worried. It's all in hand. Bye.'

Sentence commuted. A bit of pull behind the scenes. It all sounded good. So why wasn't he happy? Because the machine was in place. He'd seen it. It had a job to do. The process had started. The only logic was for that job to go ahead. Andrew didn't understand that. Safety for Riley came only from ensuring that someone else and not him accompanied Hughes and Johnson on their short walk. One of the other candidates.

A car pulled in across the street. An old dark blue BMW. A woman got out. He'd seen her coming and going before. Quite tall with long auburn hair. Wearing a tight cream sweater, long black skirt and a thick black belt. She opened the boot of her car, took out a large silver case and disappeared into her flat.

A man in a green raincoat with a flat grey cap pulled down low to shield his eyes from the drizzling rain ambled by. He paused to let his dog piss against some rubbish bags next to a lamppost. The dog, a skinny little thing, looked mournful. Obviously wishing this uncaring bastard would get him home and next to a warm fire.

A girl stood in the doorway of the grocery shop almost directly facing the flat. Riley could make out her leather jacket and jeans and the fact that her hair reached her shoulders, but that was all, since the lights of the shop cast her into gloom.

He watched the traffic lights at the end of the street go from red to green and the few cars waiting move off. A woman in a black overcoat came out of a bright red door. She disappeared round a corner.

He thought about his telephone sitting on the floor in the middle of the living room. Hoping it would ring. Wondering whom he could call.

The girl hadn't moved from the shop doorway. She must be cold. She could probably do with a coffee. She stepped out into the street and into the light as someone pushed past her into the shop. He saw that her hair was dark red and in a bob. Her right hand came out of her jacket pocket. She brushed a lock of stray hair off her cheek and behind her ear, which a single gold loop shone from. His eyes followed her hand as it dropped to her side. Each finger decorated by a gold ring. He noticed the wideness of her hips. She seemed to be staring straight at his window. The girl from the bus. He retreated into the room even though he knew there was no way she could see him. She continued to stare. The girl from the bus.

'No, it can't be.' He spoke to the walls. The walls remained silent. 'Can it?'

A car slowed to a halt next to her. Stereo blaring. Riley could only distinguish a thumping bassline. She got in and the car drove off.

He lay on the sofa, considered masturbating but switched on the TV instead. The screen blared into life and a smiling blonde happily told him which shampoo he must use regularly to avoid dandruff.

The story on the news was no story at all. A man closer to death. Frantic efforts to save a life. A crime that must be paid for. No facts. No developments. Just human interest.

'Hello.' He stopped. Frozen by a male voice. He could picture Alex standing by the telephone in their hallway. Probably with his shirt and tie on from the office. His curly black hair greyed now and receding. 'Hello.'

'Is Kath there?'

'Who? I think you've got the wrong number.'

Riley thought he sounded cagey. As if he didn't believe the wrong-number routine. Perhaps he thought he recognized the voice.

'Kathryn Potter.'

'Sorry, there's no one here with that name.'

'Sorry, I must have dialled wrong.'

'No problem.'

The phone went dead. Riley replaced the receiver. There was, of course, no way Alex could have recognized his voice. Riley hadn't spoken to him in fifteen years but it could have kicked off some sort of memory. Enough to fuel a little suspicion for him to mull over for the rest of the evening. Riley smiled. He liked that. Of course Clara wouldn't.

'Fuck her.'

'Hello.'

'Oh, hello, Anne, it's Riley.'

'Oh-oh.'

'What?'

'Well, usually when you phone it's because you don't want to see Emma.'

Shit. Sunday, he thought. This had been a mistake.

'No, I was just phoning to confirm. Make sure that it was still all right with you.'

'It is.' She sounded amused.

'Great.' He didn't know what else to say. He became mesmerized by the television screen showing a cookery programme. Deseeded red peppers glistening after being baked in olive oil. Ends curled and black.

'Hello? Are you there, Riley?'

'Yeah. I forgot where I was. Sorry, I'm losing it.' He told himself to say goodbye. But he couldn't bring himself to put the phone down. Say goodbye.

'Are you all right?'

'I'm fine, Anne.'

'What's wrong?'

'N-n-nothing.'

'I haven't heard you stammer on a word in years.'

'Not like the old days when we first met, eh? It took me about half an hour to ask you out and all I said was, "Do you fancy a coffee?"'

'That word coffee.'

'I know. Unfortunately, there aren't many substitutes for it.'

'Cappuccino?'

'That's fucking worse.'

'So what's wrong? You never talk about the past when you're happy.'

'It's nothing much. Things haven't been working out for me lately. I'm just feeling a bit down, that's all.'

'Good.'

Riley thought he had misheard. 'What?'

'Good. I'm glad. After all the crap you put me through, you expect me to sympathize. That's why you phoned, not to check on Emma. What a bloody cheek. My duty to listen to your woes finished the night you left with your suitcases. We'll see you on Sunday. By 10 at the latest. And do you want my advice?'

'Sure. Hit me with it.'

'Phone one of your girlfriends, or don't they want to know?' She hung up.

'Bitch.'

'Hello?'

'Hello. I was wondering if I could speak to Sarah please.'

'Who is calling?'

'Riley.'

'Riley.' The woman repeated his name with a hint of distaste. 'One moment.'

He could hear laughter in the background. The kind of laughter they stuck all over a sitcom on TV to try and convince you it was funny.

'Hi. This is a surprise.'

'You didn't expect me to call?'

'Of course I did, but I thought, being the ladykiller you are, you'd play it cool and wait till nearer the weekend.'

'Well, this is Mr Uncool on the line. Who answered the phone?'

'Mother.'

'She doesn't like me already.'

'She's just curious and a little protective when men she's never heard of call for me.'

'All I can say is thank goodness Dad didn't answer.'

'I'd let you speak to him but he's in the garden shed polishing his shotgun.'

'Don't bother calling him, I phoned to talk to you. How are you?'

She sighed with weariness. 'Tired. I had a shit of a day. All my fingers were thumbs, which is a real disadvantage in secretarial work. Consequently it took me three times as long to do anything. And you?'

'I've had the kind of day that one person in a million has only once in a century.'

'Sounds interesting.'

'I'd love to tell you about it. Maybe later?'

'Mmmm,' she groaned. 'Not tonight. I'm destined for a very long, very deep, very hot bath. Then bed.'

'I'd really like to see you.'

'I've got a day off tomorrow.'

'Have you?' Riley didn't want to think about tomorrow. 'I'm busy. What about in the evening?'

'Evening's fine. Give me a call about dinner-time.'

'OK.'

'And Riley.'

'What?'

'Do what I do when life gets on top of me. When you feel it's going to crush you under its' weight. Get clean. Wash it all away with water. Then get all warm and safe. Get into bed. That's where I'm going, to bed and to safety. I'll see you tomorrow. Bye.'

'Bye.'

The Girl

Riley decided that there did come a time when television bored the shit out of you. It came after hours of endless viewing. News, soap opera, German cable, weightlifting, TV movie, basketball, old soap operas, detective programmes seen a million times. Imprinted into your subconsciousness far more effectively than your seven times table ever was at school. To such an extent that you found yourself mouthing along to the lines without realizing it. Anticipating a certain character coming through a doorway at a certain time. He eventually switched off.

At 2 a.m. he sat glued to the empty streets. A taxi cruised by now and then. Through a window of an office on the corner of the block next to his he watched a cleaner moving a Hoover around for a while. A middle-aged dumpy woman with tight curly hair. She slumped herself into a swivel chair and shared tea with a man in blue overalls. A balding man. The lights had gone out at 2.15 a.m. The bathroom window looked out on to the back of the opposite block. All was dark, except for a bathroom that had briefly flashed into life. Frosted glass. A shadow hovered for a second, male or female he couldn't tell, then the whole scene disappeared into the night.

He strolled round the flat with only the streetlights to guide him and silence. He could hear the hum of his refrigerator and the click of his electricity meter every couple of minutes. He travelled from window to window. Hoping for a light or the sight of someone walking along the road. Anything to provide a second of interest.

2.40 a.m. He decided to go to the twenty-four-hour garage two blocks away and get a morning paper.

Several taxis were parked in the forecourt. Inside the drivers stood beside a collection of microwaves, drinking tea and chewing on burgers and plastic hot dogs. Doughnuts minus the hole in the middle.

The day's headline told him that interest rates had risen again. The second time this year. The economy, which earlier in the year was stronger than at any time in the previous decade, was suddenly on the slide. It was either this or the tabloid sensation that yet another footballer had been caught with his pants down, cheating on his wife. A page three model attached to him in the usual way.

He hadn't eaten since the gunge in the prison and suddenly felt hungry. He eyed the rows of chocolate bars on display. As a kid with a spot problem he'd steered clear of sweets for years, but now had a rekindled passion.

He chose a Fizz. A new bar he'd seen advertised on TV and on the side of buses. Standard milk chocolate with raisins and biscuit. Nothing to get excited about, except the biscuit contained a new chemical agent that reacted with your saliva and caused it to fizz like a foaming volcano in your mouth.

Riley decided that five years from now they'd discover that this chemical agent caused cancer, leukaemia or quickened the development of Parkinson's disease. It was probably an essential ingredient of napalm that had found a more constructive purpose. Of course, no link would ever be proved and it probably tasted damn good. He continued along the counter, picking out chocolate bars.

'What are you chewing on?' The girl beamed at him a few inches from his nose as she leaned into his face. Her breath stank of whisky.

'What?'

'I was wondering what you had chosen to eat. I've got the munchies. I need lots of chocolate and lots of sugar. Do you like these?' She held a Snickers in front of him.

'They're OK.'

'Mmmmm. I like them.' She unwrapped the bar and took a bite. 'Peanuts. Satisfying.' She followed him as he moved along the shelf. She took a chocolate bar from one of the many he carried. 'You seem to be hungry too. Am I disturbing you? Being annoying?'

Riley smiled at her. 'No, not at all.'

'Good. I have had a few drinks too many. So my judgement on how intrusive I'm being could be inextricably flawed. What are you doing out at this time of night?'

'Insomnia.'

'Chocolate won't help that.'

'I've given up on any hope of sleep. I'll eat my way through to sunrise.'

'I'm not exactly aching for sleep either. I was going home to watch TV, drink some coffee. Not the most thrilling of offers, but you're welcome to join me.'

Riley faced her fully for the first time. The slight quickening of his heart that he had tried to ignore when she first approached him and when he had first realized who she was now broke into a full sprint.

'If you want to,' she said. 'I'm only a few streets away.'

'Sure. Why not?'

All traffic had ceased. They passed an office block with every

93

light ablaze but all desks empty. Computer screens blank. Waiting for the staff to arrive before 9. Riley knew that inside some poor lonely bastard sat listening to the radio, eyelids fighting to stay open, wearing a meaningless uniform that reminded him to patrol the building at strategic intervals. Ensure its security. He headed home when everyone else went to work. He passed them in the street and not one of them knew his name but he knew some of theirs. Paused to glance at their mementoes on their desks as he made his rounds. The blonde girl he had a quiet fancy for who never registered his face as he went by. He knew that her name was Suzanne and that she had just got engaged to someone called Ian. The congratulations cards were on her desk and the sparkling ring she wore confirmed it. He laughed at his own foolishness. That she would ever be interested in a worn-out fifty-year-old widower, but he still liked to imagine her when he masturbated.

Riley recognized the street they were on as being just round the corner from his own.

A car drove slowly past them. Its speed hardly above their walking pace. It disturbed him. A car, this time in the morning, cruising past them. He tried to see in the passenger window as it moved by, but couldn't make out the occupants. It pulled into the kerb a couple of hundred yards ahead. Its engine died and so did its lights. No one got out.

Riley's steps faltered. 'That's funny.'

'What's funny?' The girl giggled. 'I think you're a bit funny.'

'No. The car.'

'What car?' She looked up the street. 'There aren't any cars.'

'The one parked ahead.'

She giggled again. 'What are you, a motor enthusiast?' She grabbed his arm and steered him to a door. 'Come on, this is us.'

Inside she put her finger to her lips to tell him to be quiet and led him by hand through the hall without turning on the light. She switched on a light in the bedroom. 'Sorry about the mess.' The floor appeared to be covered entirely with clothes. 'Just step on them. They're dirty anyway. Have a seat.' Riley couldn't see a chair. 'I'm afraid there's only the bed. I'll make some coffee.'

'Why are you whispering?'

'I don't want to wake my flatmate. She gets up early for work.' She took off her black leather jacket and laid it on a large table that held a lamp. She switched this on and turned off the ceiling light. 'That's better. I won't be a minute. Milk and sugar?'

'Just milk.'

There was a portable TV on a chair next to the bed. He turned it on and flicked channels.

The cream duvet cover had a frilly pink fringe and small pink and yellow flowers decorating it. The bed smelled of perfume. Cheap or expensive, he wasn't sure, but it had a harsh edge that caught in the throat. The mattress sagged beneath him. He piled his chocolate on top of the television and stared at the screen in the hope of diverting his attention from his erection that had kicked in as soon as they had entered the bedroom.

She must want to fuck him. Why else invite him here?

She returned just as the LA Lakers were laying siege to his attention. She placed two cups on a wooden dresser that ran along the left-hand side of the bed, spent a minute fiddling with her laces and removing her shoes before swinging her legs on to the bed and reclining. She patted the space next to her. 'Come on, you may as well get comfortable.'

Riley took his own shoes off and lay down.

Her hand rested on his thigh and she giggled. 'This is weird. I bet you didn't expect this when you popped to the shops.'

'No. I didn't.'

'Of course, it doesn't mean anything this, me inviting you back here.'

'I know.'

She giggled again. 'Bullshit. That's not what you really think. You think it's your lucky night. Some easygoing tart trying to chat you up and lure you back to her abode.'

'No.'

'Are you sure? I thought that was the general consensus on women who dared to be horny. Or dared to admit it. That they were easy.'

'No. That's a cliché.'

'Yeah, but most clichés are true.'

'Not that one. Not regarding me anyway.'

'So my reputation will be safe. I can be honest.' Her hand strayed on to his crotch. 'I do feel horny.' She started to unbutton his trousers. 'Really fucking horny.'

They kissed. Her mouth was small, with very little lip. Riley kept his eyes open. Hers were closed. He noticed a series of tiny blackheads beneath the lilac shade on her left eyelid.

Her tongue moved around energetically but failed to transmit anything to him, but her hand was a different matter. She gripped his cock firmly and stroked him slowly. As his mouth eventually responded to hers, she broke the kiss and sat over him, resting on his thighs. She continued to play with his cock. Staring into his eyes. Riley felt the ejaculation rising inside him. He made an effort to relax his buttocks. Divest himself of the pleasure.

With her other hand the redhead undid her blouse. Riley took hold of her left breast. He squeezed her nipple between his forefinger and thumb.

'Harder,' she said.

He squeezed harder. She smiled at him. He pulled himself up and put his arms around her. His hands meeting at the small of her back. They fell on to the bed on their sides and continued to kiss.

Riley undid her jeans. He wriggled his hand inside her

knickers and let his fingertips probe until he found the spot he wanted. He rubbed gently in a circular motion. Her hand took hold of his wrist and moved his hand to the left slightly.

'Just there.' She smiled again. 'That's right.'

Heat flared inside Riley. Sweat coated his body as every drop of blood within him made a mad rush to his loins. The tension releasing itself in a roll of thunder like a series of bombs carpeting an anonymous city. Filling his stomach. Sending tremors down to his knees. He stared at his cock that twitched back at him as if he had just exposed himself in a nightclub under the glare of a strobe light.

He tugged at her knickers until he had them round her ankles. He lifted himself on to her. Only the tip of his cock had entered her before he realized she was pushing him out and sliding away from him slightly.

'No, we have to stop.'

'What?'

She kissed him as if to reassure him. 'It's OK. It's just I haven't got any protection. I'm not on the pill or anything. Have you got any condoms?'

Riley could barely comprehend the question. 'Condoms? No, I haven't. I don't usually take them when I nip out for a paper.'

The redhead giggled and pulled him close to her. Kissed him. She took hold of his cock. Riley thrust with his pelvis. Trying to push through her fingers to reach the prize. She looked into his eyes. 'You'll have to pull out before you come. OK?'

Her eyes filled his.

'Yeah. Sure. I'll pull out.'

'Promise me. I don't want to be pregnant.'

'I promise.'

She guided him into her.

The core of the heat Riley felt intensified around his cock. She felt tight. The redhead lifted her arms over her head and gripped the headboard of the bed.

Riley tried to be slow, relaxed, but the heat seared through him and he thrust at her hard and quick. Before he could think, the ejaculation came. He gripped hold of her left buttock as his orgasm erupted.

As quickly as it started it finished and the heat was replaced by the cold. His legs became dead weights. He slid out of her and slumped against her side. His hand inadvertently came into contact with the sticky coating on the inside of her thighs. He wiped his fingers on his hips, realizing what he had done. He glanced at her.

Her eyes were closed. She still gripped the headboard.

'I'm sorry.'

She lashed out with her left fist and caught him on the temple but Riley didn't feel anything.

'You bastard.' She kicked out at him. 'Get away from me.'

Riley sat up and perched on the edge of the bed.

'I'm really sorry, I didn't mean to.'

The girl turned her back on him and hugged her knees. 'Get out. Get the fuck out.'

Riley dressed. He contemplated his chocolate bars, made half a motion to put them in his pocket, but decided to leave them instead. He hovered at the bed. Not sure what to do. He wanted to go home. He didn't want to leave her like this, but what could he do?

'Look, I'm really sorry. I didn't mean to come. I tried to pull out. It just happened.' The girl gave no indication of having heard him. 'If you're worried you can get a morning-after pill. This doesn't mean you're pregnant or anything. My sperm count's really crap anyway. Honest. I couldn't fertilize anything or anyone.'

The girl still didn't move.

'I am really sorry.' Riley hesitated at the door and looked at her one last time before leaving the flat.

★

The telephone woke him and sent him tumbling out of bed.

'Hello.'

'Ah, Riley.' Mr Thompson sounded bright and breezy. As if the sun had personally risen for him this morning. 'I know you're waiting on your car.'

Riley looked at his watch: 8.15 a.m.

'But it won't be coming today. There's been a little spot of bother at the prison and the warden has informed me that it would be unwise for there to be any visitors at present. I would have called earlier, but we've been trying to set up an alternative for you. That's not possible, it seems.'

Riley tasted the staleness in his mouth and fingered his shirt. Remembering why he still had his clothes on. Why he had slept so late. 'I see.'

'Well, don't sound so pleased.'

'What?'

'It means you've got the day off. You can relax and have a nice peaceful time.'

'Yeah, as long as I don't think about stretching someone's neck, I can have a lovely day.'

Riley's sarcasm failed to faze Mr Thompson. 'Take my advice and treat yourself to a trip to a museum or an art gallery. Indulge yourself in some culture. Culture can be very calming. The car will be there, as normal, at 8 tomorrow.'

'What happened at the prison?'

'It seems some of the inmates don't agree with the majority of the general public and have decided to stage a protest in the canteen. I'm assured all will be well by tomorrow.'

'OK.'

'Good. One last thing before I forget, my department has to complete a report on the progress of the death penalty system. Performance, efficiency, that sort of thing. I was wondering if you would be willing to fill out a questionnaire on how you're finding it all. It's voluntary and strictly confidential of course.

It could give us a few pointers as to how to improve our procedures for future candidates. Make life easier for them.'

'Eh, how does "Go fuck yourself" sound?'

Mr Thompson laughed. 'It sounds just about right.'

The morning news didn't have a report on the trouble at the prison, so Riley settled on the sofa to wait for the next bulletin in an hour, but his eyes closed and he drifted back to sleep before it came on.

He boiled the kettle to save time and unwrapped a disposable razor from it's plastic packaging. He poured half the water into the sink, then added some cold. The stiff bristles of the brush softened after being soaked and he worked up a creamy lather with the tin of shaving soap. He smeared the soap on to his chin and cheeks, scrubbing hard in swirls to soften his own hair. He dried his hands. Took the razor and stared into the mirror, steadying himself. This was the moment he hated. His jaw tightened, his arm stiffened, poised beside his cheek and ready to bring the blade into contact with his skin. He clenched his teeth and forced himself to do so. The soap disappeared along with the hairs and he was left with a strip of bare, slightly reddened flesh. Now that he had started, the tension in him eased. He quickly completed his cheeks and rinsed the razor.

Those were the easy parts. It was the throat and the slack skin under his jawline where the cuts occurred and the red rash and whiteheads sprouted. He took care of the area around his Adam's apple in swift upward strokes. Water ran along his arm and soaked the rolled-up sleeve of his shirt. He paused and stuck his face closer to the mirror, checking he had got all the hairs intended, but found his eyes straying to examine themselves. Only inches from their reflection. Pale blue. They flickered away as he thought of the girl he had left curled on the bed. Her skin shining in the glare from the television set. Refusing to look at him or answer his goodbye.

The telephone rang. It was the garage to tell him his car would be ready for picking up the next day.

He sat on the edge of the sofa with his towel round his shoulders, razor still in hand. Its blade covered by a film of soap and tiny hairs. A sickly sweet aroma pervaded the air. His crotch itched. He smelled of her. Her insides. He had meant to pull out. Hadn't he? But it had felt so good. Fucking her had been so good. Even now his cock stiffened at the memory. He couldn't have stopped, no matter how hard he tried. It was wrong. He knew that. It was good and it was bad. The heat and then the cold. Her voice with tears behind it. He felt cold. He needed a shower.

Susan took the parcel from him and delicately untied the red ribbon. 'What is it? What is it? What is it? I love presents.' She tore the paper apart and stared hard at the small white box. 'What's this?'

'What does it look like?'

'You were only supposed to get me chocolates.' She opened the box and took out the bottle of perfume. 'Chanel.'

'Think yourself lucky. I got paid today.'

'Thanks.' She said it quietly, uncapping the bottle and sniffing the contents.

'Good?'

'Mmmmm. I could bathe in this stuff.'

'I got a message from Andrew saying he'd be in all day and I should call by.'

'No problem. He's with someone just now but if you take a seat I'll get you in as soon as possible. Do you want some coffee?'

'Yes, thanks.'

Susan's eyebrows furrowed. 'What have you done?'

'What do you mean?'

She held the Chanel to her nose. 'You have to be feeling guilty about something.'

'Can't someone just be nice to you?' He put his most sincere and pleasant smile on his face.

'It's possible, but it's also highly unlikely. I'll get that coffee.'

He flicked through a motoring magazine. One of the many laid out on the coffee table at the leather settee. Something the redhead said came back to him. 'What are you, a motor enthusiast?' It was an odd little incident, the car passing them. No one getting out. One of a few odd little things that had happened lately. Thinking he had seen the old guy from the pub again. Even bumping into the redhead at the garage like that. He'd never seen her around before.

Susan put a mug of coffee in front of him and slumped into the settee. She sank deeper into the leather upholstery with a sigh. 'I just can't get motivated today.'

'Have some coffee. That'll perk you up.'

'No. I've got a cold coming on and caffeine kills vitamin C.' She gave him a sly glance. 'You've been in here a lot lately.'

'Have I?'

She punched him lightly on the shoulder. 'You know you have. Nothing major, I hope?' Riley drank his coffee. 'OK. Don't tell me.'

'Are you trying to make me believe you don't know everything that goes on in this office?'

'Of course I don't. I just take calls. Nobody tells me anything. Client confidentiality.'

'So you never take a quick flick through the files?'

'No.'

'I'm impressed.'

'Stop being evasive.'

He smiled at her. 'It's nothing major. The ex-wife is giving me a hard time. That's all.'

'Good. I'm glad.'

'Why?'

'Because I like you, Riley.'

'Do you?'

'Yes. I wouldn't have slept with you otherwise.'

'Well, you never mention it.'

'Neither do you. Anyway, it doesn't mean I don't like you.'

'You just didn't like "it".'

Susan sighed. 'That comment is a prime example of why I never mentioned it.' She got to her feet. 'According to biologists, people are 90 per cent water but not men. Unfortunately men are 90 per cent dick. You see, Riley, I said I liked you and you may even like me, but what you like are my tits or my arse. One day it might strike you that women are people too.'

Susan returned to her desk.

'Jesus, you look done in.'

Andrew managed a half-smile and loosened his tie. 'It's been a pretty hectic week so far. Coffee?'

'No, I've just had one. From Susan.'

'Are you friends today?'

'She doesn't believe I know that women are people.'

'And do you?'

'Sometimes. Sometimes I forget.'

Andrew poured himself some coffee. 'Number seventeen of the morning, but it's keeping me going.' He perched on the edge of his desk and sipped from his cup. 'It's not all bad news.'

'Shit.'

'Did you get my message last night?'

'Yeah.'

'That about sums everything up. Officially there is no way you can get out of being a candidate. I've explored every possibility. Unofficially it's a matter of a few words in the right ear and waiting.'

'Waiting?'

'Yes. You see, this all has to be done delicately, Riley. I'm not asking straight out and no one is going to say, "Don't worry, Andrew, we'll make sure your mate isn't the chosen one, oh and by the way you owe us a favour or two." It's more subtle than that. You're not going to be pulled out of the course, for example. You'll just not be needed come the day should Hughes be hanged.'

'You said his sentence was to be commuted.'

'I said could be commuted and it is extremely likely. It is known that he almost got the appeal and the present Home Secretary doesn't like the thought of being responsible for a man dying any more than you seem to now.'

'What do you mean?'

'Well, for God's sake, Riley, you wouldn't be in this mess if you hadn't voted for the bloody thing.' He snapped the last words out.

'I know that. I just didn't think it through properly at the time. Nobody thought it was going to pass anyway. None of the papers did. All the opinion polls said it was going to fail.'

'And you believed the papers, the pollsters?'

'Yes, I did.'

'And of course you always believe the papers.'

'No, I don't, but it seemed so absurd that people would vote to hang people and state they would do it themselves.'

'But you did. You just admitted you didn't think it out and you're a reasonably intelligent person. Why would others?'

'I know. But it's fine to say that in retrospect. I didn't think it would happen. I thought, yeah, let's get rid of the murderers, the rapists, the paedophiles, and the world will be a safer place. Children will be safer.'

'And with Hughes gone will the world be safer?'

'I don't know, Andrew, and I don't care. All I do know is that I made a monumental mistake and I need to get out of it.'

Riley walked across to the coffee machine and poured himself a cup. 'I was in the prison yesterday. I saw what is going to happen to Hughes. If you haven't seen it then you don't understand. Forget any commuting of the sentence. This thing is in motion and he is going to die.'

'You don't know that for sure.'

'I do. He's going to die. I'm positive about that. I'm also positive that I've got to get out of it. I need guarantees, so I'll ask you bluntly, how sure are you that I won't be chosen?'

'I can't give you a guarantee.'

'Percentages?'

'I'd say I was about 90 per cent sure. That's a pretty damn good percentage.'

'It's not good enough.'

Andrew brought his cup down on to the table with a crack. 'Pardon fucking me. I'm very fucking sorry that it's not fucking good enough.' He took his tie off completely, threw it on to his chair and lay down on his back on his desk.

Riley looked into the office across the street. A girl in a white blouse with short black hair intent on her computer screen.

'You really are an ungrateful bastard, Riley. I've worked fucking hard buttering people's arses I don't even like on your behalf and all you can say is it's not good enough.'

'I didn't say your efforts weren't good enough. I said the percentages weren't good enough.'

'It's the best I can do.'

'Maybe, maybe not. Maybe there is a way to get a guarantee.'

'How?'

'Maybe what is needed is more than a word.'

'Bribery?'

'A sweetener. Hear me out, Andrew. You can't tell me it doesn't go on. There isn't any corruption. I can lay my hands on quite a lot of cash.'

'You haven't got a penny.'

'There's my insurance policy. I've been paying it for years. I cashed it in a while ago and it's quite a sum.'

'You had insurance? It all sounds rather sensible for you.'

'Anne's dad started it for me when we announced her pregnancy. I stuck the money into a new account so Anne couldn't get her hands on it, thinking I'd have some savings should I run into any trouble.'

'You shouldn't do this.'

'Ninety per cent isn't enough.'

'I shouldn't do this. I'm risking everything.'

'Then you'll do it?'

'I didn't say that.'

Silence fell between them. Riley concentrated on the image of the girl across the street. The movement of her hands on a keyboard and her mouth as she talked through a headset to someone who could be just around the corner or on a different continent. He felt the silence was a giant wave that had to be ridden carefully. Taken at the correct speed and angle if he wasn't to go under. If he wasn't to drown.

He voiced his words slowly, deliberately. 'What are you saying?'

Andrew spoke quietly, as if he too anticipated the crash of the wave. 'I don't know.'

'But you do know somebody who might be willing?'

'I think so.'

Riley counted to five in his head. 'I can only ask. I've got thirty thousand. I can have it ready for this afternoon. I know it is a lot to ask, but it is literally life or death. For me, not Hughes.' He counted from five to ten. 'I'll leave and let you think about it. Let me know when you decide.'

He had almost made it to the door before Andrew reacted. 'Is that it?'

Riley turned and faced his friend. 'What do you mean?'

'Aren't you going to push all the emotional buttons? How long we've known each other. How you looked after me. Protected me. Saved me.'

'No. I'm not.'

'And what if I say no?'

Riley smiled. 'Then I'm fucked.'

The newspaper he bought had Hughes on page two. The headline stated HUGHES-DINI. The follow-up line, 'Will evil killer escape the noose?'

The Court of Appeal, after a late emotional session, rejected the plea by lawyers for Tim Hughes to be granted clemency. The three judges decided by a majority of two to one that his conviction was safe and the original sentence should stand.

The decision now rests solely with Home Secretary Howard Michaels. Mr Michaels refused to comment on the case. It is known, however, that the Home Secretary, a lukewarm supporter of capital punishment during the referendum, spent half an hour in a closed meeting with the wife of the accused and was moved by her plea.

Kerri Sayer, mother of the victim, Nancy, began a candlelit vigil last night outside the Home Office. The vigil is her attempt to prevent Mr Michaels reversing the court's decision. Surrounded by hundreds of supporters, she made her own plea for relatives of murder victims to be listened to. 'It's always the murderer people hear about. It's time the victims were given a voice. My Nancy never got any mercy from him and he doesn't deserve any from us. Britain didn't vote for mercy.'

A photograph had captured Kerri Sayer with a lit candle cupped in her hands. Its flame flaring her face. Her features like a mask hewn from marble. Ghostly eyes stared out from around her.

Fuck, Riley thought.

His office was situated on the third floor of a pebble-dashed box. 'A forbidding square of 1970s concrete stupidity' was a phrase Riley liked to use to describe it. Milo Associates had been allowed to refit the interior to suit their corporate image, but the exterior was under the protection of a heritage listing. The only clue that the firm occupied the building being a discreet plaque.

He waited across the street in the doorway of the railway station to avoid the fine drizzle spraying from an overcast sky. The weather was getting on his nerves. He wanted it to rain properly. A heavy downpour to get rid of the dour grey blanket lying over the city. He never usually noticed the weather except for the purposes of small talk.

He wondered what he was waiting for. Why was he here? Habit, he supposed. This was the place he came five sometimes six days a week. Four years he had worked for the firm. It was where he belonged. Nowhere else seemed to fit. At some point in every day he'd spent behind a desk he'd wished to have the luxury of not working at all, but at the moment he felt cast adrift. Floating away from all he knew. Surrounded by numbing silence. An astronaut whose lifeline is cut from the mothership. Given the slightest push. No resistance. No opposing force to halt his journey. The chances were he would drift for ever.

Mark, one of the sales team, and Diane scampered down the steps and turned right. They headed along the street away from Riley. He knew where they were going. The New York Coffee Company. High perched stools and a thousand different varieties of bean. He remembered his time in New York with Anne. How disappointed he had been. How tame it was. Nothing more than another fucking Disneyland really.

Riley joined the flow of commuters into the station. He stared at the departures board. The destinations barely making sense. There was nowhere to go. Nowhere except home.

Eventually it was time to call Sarah.

'Hello, Ladykiller.'

He sighed. 'I wish you wouldn't call me that. I feel I should be squeezed into a pair of leather trousers and some carefully groomed stubble.'

'Aren't you?'

'Well, I may never descend into the hell of corduroy, but no, leather isn't my thing. Sorry to let you down.'

'That's OK. Just make sure it's the last time you let me down.'

'Yes, Miss.'

'Good, so how can I help you, Mr Scott?'

'I've got an ache.'

'Really?' She sounded distressed. 'How terrible. Where is it?'

'In the heart.'

'The worst place.'

'Can you help?'

'No, sorry, I've got a date.'

'Oh.' Riley fingered the telephone cable, feeling stupid. The only blessing was she couldn't see him. 'I see.'

'Yes, I'm going to someone's flat with a couple of bottles of wine.' She sounded so bloody chirpy. 'I'm really looking forward to it.'

'Good.'

'The only trouble is, the idiot hasn't told me his address yet.'

It took a second for the meaning of her words to penetrate the irritation surrounding him. The irritation evaporated into a smile.

She arrived as promised with wine. Riley had popped out and bought a couple of bottles as well. They both sat on the edge of the settee. He'd put a CD on, but it didn't seem to have the right effect. It didn't bring them together. It only seemed to emphasize the fact that the two of them were alone in the room. It left an atmosphere of soullessness hanging in the air like a sparsely populated nightclub. Their conversation evolved in short fractured bursts until it eventually deserted them.

He drank his wine and noticed Sarah smiling into her glass. 'What are you smiling at?' he asked.

'I was just thinking that this is the awkward time.'

'What do you mean?'

'You know, when we're both wondering what will happen. When are we going to kiss? Am I going to stay the night? Do you want me to stay the night? The awkward time.'

'I guess I've just got used to having sex. I'm out of practise with relationships. That sounds terrible, but at least you now know I'm no ladykiller. This proves it.' Sarah giggled. 'I'm pretty sure Casanova would have had a smoother line in chat than I've got. Don't you think so?'

'Maybe.' She stood up and held her hand out to him. 'Let's go and lie down.'

'What?'

'I want to lie down. I want you to hold me. That's all. I want to feel close to you. You see, I like you, Riley, a lot, but I want to know if I like being near you.'

'It's a test then?'

She frowned. 'Don't mock. Just take my hand.'

They undressed with their backs to each other and slid into opposite sides of the bed. She pushed his shoulder round until his back was to her, then wrapped her arm around his waist. They lay in the dark saying nothing. Riley blinked up into the stars outside the window, listening to the traffic pass by. Now and then voices could be heard. Laughter. The odd burst of singing. People going to or coming back from the pub. The minutes ticked by on the red face of the clock. Her skin lay on his with the warmth of water freshly poured for the bath. He felt it cleansing him. He reached round and stroked her thigh. She lifted her leg slightly and draped it across his so their toes were almost touching. She rubbed gently with her thumb on his stomach.

'So how does it feel,' he whispered, 'to be close to me?'

She kissed the back of his neck lightly. 'It feels nice. Quite stimulating actually.'

'Thank God for that.' Her laughter transmitted itself through the rumble of her stomach into his back. He swivelled round to face her. Her emerald eyes beaming at him. Shining through the darkness. 'I'm glad.'

She smiled at him and they kissed.

The Prisoner

It took him a little time to realize he was at home and in his own bed. Years had passed without him waking next to another person minus the bad breath and the clammy sweat from the previous night's alcohol.

The clock told him it was a little after 7. Sarah lay with her back to him. Her head buried into her chest and the duvet clasped close to her chin. Her body emanated the sweet smell of baby powder and perfume. Riley fingered the floral-patterned cover on the duvet and tried to remember the last time he had changed it or washed it and any of the sheets.

Rain fell on the streets from a drab pale grey sky. Riley watched the first stirrings of city life while drinking his coffee.

A white front door to one of the houses opposite opened and a thin middle-aged balding man appeared. He carried a strange object on to the pavement and began to unfold it. It arranged into a wheelchair. He disappeared back into the house. Rain fell on to the empty chair.

A man in a grey double-breasted suit stepped out of the shop from which Riley had spotted the redhead the other night. He carried a briefcase and was trying to shove the day's paper inside his jacket to stop it getting wet.

Riley laughed. 'Put it in your briefcase, you silly bastard.'

The wheelchair man struggled down the steps carrying a large woman with long dark hair. He settled her in the chair and she unclasped her arms from around his neck. Riley had seen her before. Coming and going from the house. Walking. Before he could wonder too much about what had happened to her, his telephone rang. He felt caught between not wanting the ringing to disturb Sarah and not wanting to answer it. Only one person rang at this time of day.

'Hello.' He said it tentatively.

'The deal's done.'

It took him a second to comprehend the meaning of Andrew's words.

'Are there any questions I should be asking, Andrew?'

'How much, when and where are good questions to ask, Riley, but how or who is better left alone.'

'OK.' Riley kept his euphoria deep in his gut. Far from his voice. He'd let it out later. 'How much?'

'Twenty thousand. That still leaves you a sum in the bank.'

'Yeah, it does. Great. When and where?'

'My office. Tomorrow at 11.'

'But I'll be at the prison, on the course.'

'No, you won't.'

'What do you mean?'

'My source is, by nature, close to this. You'll be told today that you won't have to be at the prison tomorrow until 5 at night. That's twelve hours before Hughes is due to hang.'

'That soon? Oh, God, yeah, Sunday.'

Andrew sighed. 'I'd have thought you'd at least have kept track of time, Riley.'

'I thought he was going to be done on Sunday night. Midnight or something. They told me on Monday I was on this course for a week. What a load of bullshit.'

'Well, you didn't expect them to tell you the truth, did you?'

'Actually I did. I guess that's pretty stupid.'

'Yes, it is.'

Riley didn't know what to say now. Should he say, 'Thanks'? Did it change what was between them? Andrew could have risked his career, or had he done it before?

'Do you think I've wasted my money, Andrew?'

'I don't know. I still think Hughes'll get commuted and serve life, but I suppose none of that matters to you now. You've got your guarantee.'

'What should I say to you, Andrew?'

'Don't say anything at all.'

Riley stretched out on his carpet and surveyed the uneven surface of his ceiling. He could breathe again. He still had to face the prison, but he could breathe again.

Sarah loomed into view. Standing over him. 'What are you grinning at?'

'Just happy.'

She knelt beside him and kissed his cheek. 'I'm feeling kinda happy too.'

'Good.'

'Coffee?'

'Tea. Coffee sends me straight to the loo in the morning.'

He made tea as she got dressed and they sat together on the two-seater settee.

'Do you like living here, Riley?'

'I don't know.'

He looked at the cream walls that he had somehow never got round to hanging anything on. The small square wicker table with the paraffin lamp on top. The only two items, apart from his books, that he'd taken from the family home. Anne had held on viciously to the wedding presents. Even the ones from his side of the family. The two plants that had been in the flat when he'd arrived. Although not flourishing, he had kept them alive. A TV borrowed from a friend. Four years later still in his possession.

'I don't know. I haven't really thought about it much. When I split with my wife it was a convenient place to move into. It was available and not too expensive. I had planned to buy a two-bedroom flat as soon as I got some money together but my maintenance payments and the legal fees from the divorce scuppered that. And I suppose, to tell the truth, I'm not the best of savers, I tend to spend what I've got, but I'd still like to move on so my daughter has a room to stay in.'

'So where does she sleep when she stays?'

'In the bed. I crash on this.' He patted the settee. 'But she doesn't stay much.'

'Why?'

'I don't know. It's just the way things have worked out.' He felt uncomfortable with this because he knew it was a lie. 'Anyway, what are you doing this evening?'

She smiled. 'Seeing you.'

'Oh, really?'

'Yes.'

'You seem very sure of yourself, Miss.' The buzzer to the front door went. 'That'll be my lift.'

Sarah rose with him and followed him through to the hall. 'Shouldn't I be sure of myself?'

'Of course you should. Just make sure the door is locked when you leave. Shall I give you a call later?'

'No. I'll call you after work. OK?'

They kissed.

'OK.'

'It's not exactly what I expected.' Riley's voice echoed his thoughts around the white steel-walled room. He peered above, to where the ceiling was barely visible through the gloom. The white panels of the walls were separated by streaks of bright orange and dark brown rust. The result of condensation seeping between the join of rivet and steel.

'It's as good as anywhere.'

Mr Johnson dumped the coil of rope round his shoulder on to the floor. A dull clang greeted its arrival. He wore an old pair of denims strapped at the waist with a thick leather belt and a checked woollen shirt. He rolled his sleeves to the elbow, then grabbed the leather bag that Riley had carried into the room.

In Riley's eyes he could pass for any workman you saw on a construction site. Half mooning at you whenever he bent over.

Riley wore a pair of overalls that Johnson had managed to scrounge for him off a guard. Black overalls. Two sizes too big. He'd had to roll the sleeves just to find his hands in them. 'Are you sure I have to wear this?' He tugged at the top of the overalls and knew he sounded like a schoolboy being forced into his new blazer and tie before school.

'There's a lot of oil and shit around here. It's up to you.'

Johnson switched on fluorescent strips and the structure that Riley knew when they entered to be the gallows was struck with bright light. A man stood on the gallows.

'Who's that?'

'That's Mike. He's a nice guy. Very quiet.' Johnson smiled at Riley grimly. 'He's who we're hanging today.'

The ceiling was now clearly visible and a good forty feet above them. They had taken an elevator down to the ship's engine room to reach this level.

'This used to be part of the cargo hold. There's a small holding cell next door that's right beside the actual engines.' Johnson walked to the gallows, not indicating whether Riley should follow or not. 'Of course, it's all run down now. You'd be lucky to make it further than the shore with the turbines left on the boat, but it's enough to keep her steady in a storm. Well, enough as long as she's attached to her anchor. Hughes'll be brought down to the cell the night before. Stand under the platform.'

Riley did as he was told. The underside of the gallows was only a few feet from his upturned face. He reached on tiptoe and managed to brush his fingertips against its surface. Unvarnished new timber. Its smell strong enough to overpower the diesel fumes.

It was dark under the gallows platform. He could hear Johnson shuffling around above him. He stared out into the harsh light of the cargo hold and felt like a rat waiting for the big people to pass by. What the fuck was Johnson doing? Riley heard the sound of timber splitting. The ground vibrated beneath his feet. A pillar next to him shuddered. He realized the gallows were collapsing and threw himself to the floor. Arm raised to protect his head from the wood he expected to come crashing in on him. Instead, Mr Johnson peered at Riley curiously through a square hole in the platform. His white hair glowing as if being attacked by a cold weather front. Threatening an imminent flurry of snow.

'That's the trap door.'

Mike said nothing and his expression refused to reveal his thoughts. It perturbed Riley, since he was about to send him hurtling into God's or someone else's capable hands. He eventually managed to pull the hood over the dummy's head and stepped to the side. He slid out the metal pin that fastened the wooden handle to the gallows frame. He gripped the handle with both hands. Johnson adjusted the noose. He took a half-step back and nodded. Riley pushed the handle down and himself into darkness. His heart fell like a stone dropped from a bridge and only the smack of the trap door stopped it from falling from him completely. The noise didn't shake him as badly as when he'd been below it.

A voice spoke close to his ear. 'You'll find it easier if you keep your eyes open.'

Riley opened his eyes. He followed Johnson to the edge of

the trap door. They looked down on the hooded figure suspended in the air.

'That's more or less what you'll see. It's not so bad, is it?'

'I guess not.'

Johnson examined a stopwatch round his neck. 'Not bad for a first effort, but we'll have to put a pile of work in this morning.'

'What about the other candidates? Who trains them?'

Johnson started hauling Mike up through the trap door. 'Me. You're all done at different times. I'll be with one of the others this afternoon.'

'What'll I be doing?'

'I really don't know.'

'What are the other two like?'

Johnson removed the hood from Mike's head and passed it to Riley. 'You ask a lot of questions, Mr Scott.'

'You can't blame me for being curious.'

'I guess not. I've no comment on anyone on the course. Sorry. Regulations.' Johnson worked the rope free and loosened the noose. 'I'm also sorry about the overalls. I should have told you to bring some old clothes.'

'Don't worry.'

'Before I forget, have you got a suit?'

'Of course I've got suits.'

'Wear one on Saturday just in case it's you. It's a bit more dignified to wear a suit and a tie. A dark tie. Not black mind you, that's a touch too morbid.'

'But not too flowery? Something tasteful.'

'Exactly.'

'No problem.'

The shock of the figure falling and the squeal of the handle as its gears worked the trap door open faded into insignificance the more times they carried out the mock hanging. Johnson showed Riley where to stand. Positioned him at certain points during the procedure until Riley felt no more of a real person than Mike. They practised ascending the stairs of the gallows slowly. Leg strap. Hood. Noose. Adjust. Push.

Eventually, like Johnson, Riley became caught in their times. A few seconds quicker felt like a triumph. No sooner was Mike striking the end of the rope than Riley was anxiously consulting the stopwatch.

Again and again they went through the motions until Riley lost interest and Johnson became satisfied.

They sat side by side. Legs dangling over the edge of the platform. Each with a cup of coffee from a flask Johnson dug out of his bag. Johnson stared down through his feet, as if his vision could pierce the metal floor and peer into the deep of the sea.

'Why is the dummy called Mike?'

Johnson smiled. 'I named him after a sergeant I had when I first joined the army. He was a complete bastard. I'd love to get him on the end of a rope. I guess that doesn't sound very humane, but he didn't inspire much humanity in me. I know the army isn't about humanity. It's about teaching people to kill others. I also know, from experience, that training recruits isn't for the faint-hearted. It's tough work. But it's no excuse for being a brutal sadist. He must have dished out more senseless beatings on helpless teenagers than your average whore gives blow jobs in a career.'

'What happened to him?'

'I don't know. He probably retired and became someone's lovable grandad. I used to dream about meeting him some day. Giving him some justice. Now I watch him taking the drop. How about you? Who would you like to hang?'

'I don't know. Different people at different times.'

'What about now?'

Several faces passed through Riley's mind. One more than others. 'James Thompson.'

'Who's he?'

'The cunt who called me up for this course.'

Johnson patted him on the thigh. 'I hate to tell you, buddy, but you called yourself up for this.' Johnson reached into his pocket and offered Riley a mint.

Riley crunched into the hard boiled sweet. 'That's something I'm just beginning to accept. What about you? Why are you here?'

Johnson rubbed with his thumb at a streak of dirt on the leg of his trousers. 'Oh, I don't really know to be honest. I worked for the Addison Corporation before this.'

'What's the Addison Corporation?'

'They run the prisons. After the government got sick of dealing with the criminal population, they put the job out to tender. Addison won the contract. I started training the guards but I got bored with it. It was too much like the army. After twenty years I'd had enough of uniforms and discipline. So when this opening came up I applied.'

'You and how many others?'

'You'd be surprised. There were a lot.'

'Have you ever done anything like this before?'

Johnson pawed at an itch behind his left ear. 'What, hang someone or just generally do a bit of killing?'

'Either.'

'I experienced combat in the army and I did take lives, but that was different, that was fighting. It's nothing like this. What I said to you the other day is true. We're just mechanics. Society's already killed these people. That's what the death penalty is, not me or you but society as a whole saying that these types of people do not deserve to live among us. And let's face it, who would argue? These people are getting off lightly. There's little suffering. A lot less than their victims went through. I have no sympathy for them. Not one drop.' Johnson screwed the plastic cap on to his Thermos and returned it to his bag. 'I have to say our times are looking pretty impressive, but I think we better stick in another couple of hours and see if we can shave another second or two off. Come on, let's go give your friend Jim a ride on the big swing.'

By the end of the morning Riley had grown totally immune to his surroundings. He had lost his discomfort at touching things. The rope, the hood, the handle he had to push. He could even manhandle Mike and remove the noose from his neck. His only irritation was a splinter that refused to budge from the knuckle of his forefinger. Riley asked himself if his feelings were due to his dealing only with a dummy, or because he knew he wasn't going to be around at the actual event. The other possibility couldn't be true. Hanging wasn't so bad. Like Johnson said, it was really just a job. The state had effectively already killed the man. The two of them were just the mechanics.

Mr Lewis called for him at lunch-time and escorted him to the canteen. They rode the elevator together, Lewis fiddling with a file of papers.

'Everything OK?' he asked.

'Sure.' Riley decided a standard question deserved a standard reply.

'I'm afraid you'll have to dine alone.' He flourished his files. 'Life is a mountain of paperwork at the moment.'

'More like you can't face the food.'

'I have to confess that there are an apple and a sandwich nestling invitingly in my briefcase.'

'How's things here? I heard there was a spot of bother.'

'Yes, some of the natives got excited with the impending departure of Mr Hughes. Speaking of which, you won't be due here until 5 tomorrow. A car will pick you up at your house around 4. The final selection, if still required, will be made about 1 a.m.'

'Can I bring my own car?'

Lewis nodded his head. 'I don't see why not, as long as we have someone escort you.'

'It's just in case I'm picked. I'm having my daughter on Sunday, so I'd need to drive over there when we're finished.'

'Sure. I understand. You've got a girl?'

'Yeah.'

'I've got kids.'

Riley decided not to take the conversation any further.

The canteen was empty except for a solitary diner. Riley carried his tray of fish pie with frozen peas, stodgy rhubarb crumble and custard towards him. What else could he do? Be a rude bastard and sit at the other end of the room?

'Do you mind if I sit here?'

The man barely glanced at him and then nodded his head to indicate he had no objection. Riley took the seat opposite him.

The fish pie started growing in Riley's mouth instead of diminishing when he chewed it. The more he chewed the larger it got. His cheeks bulged with flakes of rubbery cod and lumpy mashed potato. The cheese topping had the same texture as the plastic sheeting with little air bubbles that shops wrapped delicate objects with. A few forkfuls were enough. His spoon barely made a dent on the crust of the rhubarb crumble. He slid the tray aside and nursed his coffee.

His companion grinned. 'Not hungry, eh?'

Riley grinned back. 'Had a big breakfast this morning.'

'At least as a taxpayer you know your money isn't being wasted.'

'Who says I pay my taxes?'

'A fellow criminal then.' The man stared at Riley, waiting to see if his statement had any impact.

'You're a prisoner?'

'That's right. That's what my blue overalls mean.'

The man's piercing blue eyes sparkled beneath arched black eyebrows. Sunken cheeks. Straight nose and thin lips. Framed with long silver hair. The man scratched his chin and Riley saw the strap around his wrist with a number printed in red on it. The face reminded Riley of someone. Somewhere.

The TV shop. The girl asking if she could help him. His lack of response because he was too engrossed in the story. Asking her to turn the volume up. The newscaster. The portrait over his shoulder. Tim Hughes. This was Tim Hughes. But it couldn't be. They wouldn't allow them to meet. They wouldn't even allow him to be sitting on his own.

Hughes seemed to read his thoughts. 'Don't worry, we're not alone. We're being watched every second.' He pointed above himself. 'Eye in the sky. The entire prison is covered with them. Half the guards never meet a prisoner. They're glued to the CCTV screen. Of course, that's no real comfort. I mean, if I was the violent type, I could easily stick a fork in your eye before anyone came running to the rescue, but that's forgetting about this.' Hughes tapped the band on his wrist. 'One silly move and this bugger lets loose enough electricity to paralyse me and leave my gonads tingling for a good while after. So relax. I'd like you to stay. That's if the smell of a criminal doesn't disturb you. Most people seem to think we stink like shit. How we've evolved in two thousand years.' He looked at Riley with a hint of sadness behind his eyes. 'I haven't had many conversations lately and the ones I have had have all been about the same thing.'

'So what makes you think I'm not a prisoner?'

'The obvious. The overalls. In case you haven't noticed, mine are blue and they're blue for a reason. Besides, you haven't the look. And of course there is one other reason.'

'What's that?'

Hughes pointed his forefinger at a spot between Riley's eyes. 'I know who you are.'

Riley didn't want to ask the question but had to. 'So who am I?'

'You're the good citizen they're training to hang me.' Shock hit Riley's face. Its impact made Hughes happy and his face beamed with delight. 'Don't worry, I forgive you.'

'It might not be me. It might be one of the others.'

This revelation reduced Hughes to laughter and tears. It took him a moment to calm himself and respond. 'Oh, yes, the others, I forgot about them. I'm afraid not. You're going to have to come to terms with a very simple fact.'

'What fact?'

'It is going to be you. Yours will be the last face that I ever see.'

'You don't know that.'

'I do. I've seen it happen.'

It was Riley's turn to laugh. 'What are you? Psychic?'

'You don't have to be psychic to see the future. When I go back to my cell with its blank white walls, I've got nothing to look at. All I can see out of the tiny square window near the roof is the sky and that doesn't change much. You can pretty much guarantee it's going to be grey. So all I do is think. I stretch out on the paper-thin mattress that pretends to be a bed and I lay my head on the damp pillow that smells of grease and sweat and I close my eyes. I think. It's the only way I can get out of this place. I've been doing it for eleven months. Three hundred and forty-eight days. Twenty-three hours a day in a cell. Seven thousand, nine hundred and fifty-eight hours. For most folks that would constitute a lifetime's thinking.' Tim Hughes sipped his by now cold coffee and rubbed the dark shadows beneath his eyes. 'I guess for me you'd be able to say the same.'

Riley noticed for the first time the washed-out pallor of his skin. An almost lifeless quality emanated from the man.

'Of course, I started off pondering the present. The trial and the sentence. In my mind I searched every line on the faces of the people involved. Every word that they uttered. I went over and over what was said, who said it, when it was said. My wife, the lawyer, witnesses and the jury. I studied it all with the abstract notion of understanding whether these were the right people in my life at the right time. Did they all fit or was there one who shouldn't have been around? The reason why I had ended up like this. Had I married the right woman, for example? If I had married the girl I had been seeing previously, would it all have turned out differently? Why was I here? Had I said the wrong thing at the wrong time? Why am I going to die?

You go round and round the events, the evidence. It's the kind of questioning that eventually drives you crazy. It drove me crazy almost as much as the police did. You see, there isn't any answer to it except the inevitable one that whatever will be will be. You are what you are. Who, what, why and when are all circumstantial.'

'Are you trying to say that people can't affect their own future? Because if you are, that's bullshit.'

'I'm not saying that. All I'm saying is the end result will always be the same.'

'To me that's a convenient excuse for not taking responsibility. You're saying that you had no choice. You were destined to kill Nancy.'

'No. It doesn't matter which choices I made, I would still have come to this point, and so would you.'

'I don't see that. I'm here by a quirk of fate. You're here for murder.'

'Voting for the death penalty could hardly be described as a quirk of fate.'

Riley took a drink from his own lukewarm cup.

'Anyway, as I was saying, questions about the present, the trial and ending up here were only proving destructive, so I started thinking about the past. It's amazing how much I'd forgotten about growing up. School. Family history. University. Whole stretches of my life were blank. University is a good example. In my second and third years I'd shared a house with three other students and I couldn't recall anything about it. What we'd done. If we'd gone about together. It took me an hour to remember their full names and put a face to those names.

'Childhood was worse. Certain incidents were sharp and fresh in my mind. For example, when I was about three the family went on a holiday to Scarborough. My dad drove in an old Hillman Imp. A tiny white car. There was something wrong with the car and we kept stopping almost every half-hour. The engine mushrooming a cloud of steam. Dad pouring water into it. It was a nightmare journey but eventually we got there and it was the first time I'd ever seen the sea. It sparkled at me like a lake of delicious fizzy pop and I ran straight for it as soon as my dad had let go of my hand. I hit the water at high speed and the sea filled my eyes, ears and mouth. I remember the shock that it didn't taste sweet, but I kept going forward. My dad had to come in after me. He was so scared, he didn't even have time to take off his shoes. His suit was soaked as he fished me out. A suit he had recently bought. He used to claim that he could never wear it afterwards because, no matter what they did to it, it still smelled of the sea.

'Of course the question is, do I remember this incident or have I been told the story so many times that I've committed it to memory? Probably the latter. It's not the actual events but a version of the events. Not any more. Because I've made the effort to remember. I haven't been told anything. I can now remember what my life was like on a daily basis. How I felt. How certain incidents affected me. What choices I made or had made for me. Sometimes, night or day, it's only a relative difference to me at the moment, I can run through my mind the face of my mother or my father from when I was very young to the present. It's an extraordinary image. Like one of those computer-generated things you see on television now and then, or film speeded up of a flower growing. Eyebrows changing shape, sprouting new hairs, grey hairs, blonde hairs. The ends lengthening and curling. My dad's chin expanding. Losing its definition. Bags filling beneath his eyes. Even earlobes sagging slightly as if they didn't have the strength to continue to hang there any longer.

'Now when I think back to my sprint into the sea I know it's for real. I can feel the anticipation of drinking in the blue fizzy pop. The realization as it seeps into my mouth. Lying on my bunk, I can taste the salt. Feel it washing over my face.'

'It's a beautiful story, but what's this got to do with me?'

'It's simple. There's no great divide between the past and the future. They are in a sense interchangeable. You see, as well as seeing every day of my past, I have also seen the future. Not literally but when I look at you. I know you are the one. I have felt the final day.' Riley shifted his eyes from the fixed gaze of Tim Hughes. 'I know it sounds crazy, but I have seen it, and deep down you know it's true, because you have seen it as well.'

'No, I haven't.'

'Then it's because you've locked it away inside.' Hughes tapped his chest and Riley felt he could hear the rush of blood that his heart pumped through his body. 'You have to take time to look for the future, and when you find it you'll discover that it all comes down to you and me.'

'You're wrong.'

'Am I?' Hughes laughed and spread his arms, as if welcoming someone he hadn't seen for a long time. 'Then what are we two doing sitting here? Is it just coincidence?'

'You must be due to meet the other candidates.'

'Oh, I suppose I am. I don't really know, though, they don't consult me on the schedule.'

'It could be one of them.'

'But I haven't seen them in the future, Riley. I've only seen you putting a white hood over my head.'

A guard entered the canteen and strode towards them.

It was a ploy. Riley knew it. Hughes was only trying to upset him. But it was a ploy that was working.

'You're talking shite, Hughes. Nobody can see the future.'

The guard touched Hughes on the shoulder. 'Come on, Tim, lunch is over.'

Hughes got to his feet, his smile never leaving Riley. 'I know everything. I see everything.'

The guard led him away.

Riley stared at the dregs of his coffee. 'Nobody can see the future.' He shivered at a sudden thought and dropped the cup back on to its saucer. He shouted at the departing prisoner, 'How the fuck do you know my name?'

Hughes glanced over his shoulder. His grin still in place. 'I told you, Riley, I know everything.'

The guard ushered him on through the canteen doors, which swung twice then closed.

This was bullshit. All of it. He had a guarantee. Twenty fucking grand's worth. How did Hughes know his name? He'd been guaranteed anonymity. Perhaps it could be a way out without spending a penny. His anonymity had been compromised. Surely that meant he'd have to be pulled off the course. It sounded good. Real good. He could hardly wait to see Thompson's fucking face.

No one came to fetch him and take him somewhere else. His watch said 2.45. There didn't seem to be anything to stop him walking out and wandering off round the prison if he felt like it, but he remained seated. Puzzled by what had taken place. Presumably Hughes would use the same story to goad the other candidates. The use of the name had been good, though, the way he'd dropped it in. How had he known? Thompson? It might be logical to assume he knew the other candidates' names if he had been told Riley's. So everyone's anonymity had gone. The hanging could not take place until new candidates were chosen, or perhaps there wasn't going to be a hanging. A life sentence instead. It still didn't make sense. Hughes would still know the names of those involved.

Riley fetched himself another coffee from the self-service machine at the counter.

Only one answer made sense. He sipped from his cup. The hot liquid stinging his lips. The crash of the trap door echoed through his head.

Thank God for Andrew.

The garage had valeted the car's interior and it smelled of air freshener and carpet cleaner. As impersonal as a chain hotel room in any city in the world. He opened his glove compartment, half expecting to find a Gideon's Bible, but was reassured to find his half-used packet of mints. He popped a mint into his mouth and sat watching customers from the shopping mall they were under come and go.

His life savings rested on his knees. Maybe he should be grateful, he had been prepared to hand over the full thirty and had even withdrawn the whole amount without thinking. He shoved the money back into the padded envelope and dropped it on the passenger seat. He could have done a runner with thirty thousand. Getting out of the country might have been a problem, but he could probably have found a way. But where would he have gone? Anywhere. What was there to stay for? Clara? That was going nowhere. His parents were fast becoming a distant memory. Anne didn't give a shit. If he was to become a memory, who would really miss him? Emma? Riley paused. What a horrible thought. Wondering if your daughter would actually miss you. But what had he given her for the past few years? The conversation with Sarah about his daughter had unsettled him. He hadn't seen that much of her because he had taken the easy option too many times. The temptation to go to the pub, to play football, to make excuses. All he had given her was very little time.

He thought about what Hughes had said. Remembering every day. Going through it all step by step. Did it really tell you anything? Surely it all came down to choices made, and the frightening aspect of life was how much of it tended just to happen. How few choices he had actually made. Having a baby. Getting a job. Going to university. These details seemed to enter his life without him actively seeking them out.

Maybe Hughes was right. Who you married, where you lived, it was all circumstantial. The real world existed inside you and real life was how it decided to come out of you. On that basis, what choices had he made? Sleeping with someone else while married. Conscious choice or had it just happened? He didn't know. Voting for the death penalty? That was one he didn't want to contemplate.

A car swung into the bay next to his. A middle-aged couple got out. The woman with short blonde hair and steel-rimmed spectacles peered in his passenger window at him suspiciously before moving off to the elevator. The elevator doors opened and a woman with a pushchair emerged from the square of dull yellow light. The couple got in and the doors closed.

Riley wondered who Andrew had got in contact with for the bribe. Thompson had been well dressed for a civil servant. Perhaps he liked to top up his salary. It didn't matter. All that mattered was that Andrew had come through when he needed him. Strangely, his friendship with Andrew could be counted as one of the few conscious decisions he had ever made. All he had to do was close his eyes and once again he was stumbling home on that cold night. Stumbling because it had been a long night on the piss. Crossing the park that lay between his flat and the university campus, he thought he heard a muffled shout. It may not have been the first. He'd probably been too engrossed in the rich flavours of his shish kebab to notice any others. He stopped and turned round, guessing the noise had come from behind him, but the concrete path was empty. Only a slight drizzle and his warm breath to see. Another shout. This one with the edge of a scream to it. It seemed to come more from his side beyond the illumination of the streetlights. From the black expanse of grass that people sunbathed on in the summer months. A third shout and Riley found himself running into the black. Either his eyes adjusted extremely quickly or God had guided him. Within a few yards he could make out two figures writhing together on the ground. He pounded on towards them. One figure lay on top of the other. Their arms appeared locked. Riley could hear their breathing as they struggled. Grunts, gasps of air gulped down. Pigs at the trough. Riley grabbed the shoulders of the figure on top. The person swung an arm at him. The blow not strong enough to hurt but enough to throw him off balance. By the time Riley steadied himself, he faced a man wearing a combat jacket and a balaclava and carrying a knife.

He realized now what a blessing it was being pissed. He never flinched. Sober he'd have filled his trousers. Instead he fixed on the pair of dark eyes staring at him. Silently urging the fucker on. The pair hung suspended for a moment until Mr Balaclava accepted the challenge and leapt at him. Riley jumped aside. Tumbling to the ground. By the time he'd gathered his senses Mr Balaclava had disappeared into the darkness.

Riley clung on to the grass and drank in the smell of the soil until he remembered how many dogs tended to shit in the park and got up. The second figure still lay on the ground, on his stomach. Riley touched his shoulder.

'Are you all right?'

A face looked out over its shoulder at him. The tear-stained face of a young boy he vaguely recognized. The boy could say little and it wasn't until Riley took him back to his flat and had him settled in a hot bath that he remembered who he was. Where he'd seen his face before. On the front cover of the first edition of the year of the student magazine. The article welcoming the youngest ever undergraduate to the university. Fourteen-year-old Andrew Garwood. Genius. Eight straight A-levels, studying law.

Riley made some coffee and took it in to Andrew, who sat, arms hugging knees, facing the surface of the whitened soapy water of the bath.

'Hope you like your coffee black. I haven't any milk.'

Andrew didn't react.

'So you're the child prodigy. How's law?'

'Still fallible.'

'Don't worry, you'll change all that. Listen, once you're out and dried, I'll phone you a taxi. I guess your parents will want to call the police. Shall I ring them? They must be worried about you. They might want to come and get you.'

'They're in Brussels.'

'Oh, right. Who do you want me to call?'

'No one, it's all right. I'll be fine in a taxi.'

'Who are you staying with?'

'I've got a room in the halls of residence.'

'For the term?'

'Yeah.'

Riley couldn't believe it. He'd lived in the halls himself for a year and remembered it as a place were everyone got blitzed on cheap beer, high on whatever drug they could get a hold of and fucked everyone else. What kind of fucking parents pissed off and left their kid behind? Andrew must have read his thoughts.

'It wasn't their idea. I insisted. I wanted to see a bit of the world. Look, if they hear about this they'll drag me back home and I really don't want that. I mean, I'm OK. No harm done, as the cliché goes.'

He looked again at the kid sitting in the bath. He didn't even look fourteen. Short, skinny, bony. He looked to be nearer ten or twelve. Poor bastard. It was then he decided to look after the kid. A conscious decision. It hadn't just happened. He'd stuck him in some clothes, taken him home, offered to call the police, then promised to meet him in the student union the next day. He hadn't promised because of guilt or pity or through coercion. He'd promised because he'd wanted to. Because he'd wanted Andrew to be all right.

They'd only ever spoken about the night they met once. The next day in the union. Andrew told him how he'd left the halls and taken a short cut to a twenty-four-hour garage to get some chocolate. A much-needed sugar rush to finish an essay. On the way the masked man had jumped him. Andrew didn't cry telling this to Riley, who was the one who didn't want to know. Who didn't want to face the masked man again. Whether he was after his arse or his wallet, Riley didn't ask, but he couldn't believe the naïvety of the kid or the stupidity of his parents.

'Stay away from that park at night, kid. It's a bit of a cruising district and a few people have been jumped there. I don't normally cross it at night unless I'm out of my face. Which I was last night.'

Riley made sure in the two years he had left that Andrew was included and that he always had an idea of where he was. He smiled to himself. In some way it had all paid off. Being a Christian was a good thing after all.

A knock on the window of the car stirred him out of his

memories. A face crowned with a peaked cap was squinting through the glass at him. Riley lowered the window.

'Hello?'

A cloud of stale air from the security guard's mouth reached Riley before his words. 'Can I ask you what you're doing, sir?'

'What?'

The guard glanced round the inside of the car, eyes momentarily settling on the padded envelope on the passenger's seat. 'We've had a report of someone acting suspiciously on this level of the car park. Are you waiting on someone?'

'No.'

'I see.' The guard slowly thought this over. Eyes flicking from Riley to the rows of cars beyond him. 'I guess you'll be moving on soon?'

'When I'm ready.'

He looked Riley in the eye and nodded before straightening up. He turned to leave.

'Aren't you going to ask me if I've seen someone suspicious?'

The security guard halted. 'No, sir, that's all right. I've thoroughly checked this level.'

As he walked to the elevators, Riley saw him whispering into his radio. Neck crooked, head down. The elevator arrived and he stepped in.

Riley started his car. 'Fuck's sake.'

He had barely got through his front door when the buzzer went. The noise, although familiar, startled him, like a dentist's drill making contact.

'Shit.'

He wasn't expecting anyone. It went again in short, sharp bursts. Whoever it was could've seen him come in. He'd have to answer it. He shoved his thirty grand under the settee and steadied himself before lifting the receiver.

'Hello?'

'It's me.'

The word fuck flooded from his brain, through his body and down to the soles of his feet.

'Come in.'

He left his door open and waited for her by the window. She hovered in the doorway. Her hands jammed down in the pockets of her black raincoat. Large sunglasses hiding her eyes.

'Hello, Clara.'

'Hi.'

'I don't think that disguise is going to fool anyone.' He'd said it jokingly, but her grim expression never flickered.

'It's not a disguise, it's to hide the bruises.'

She removed the sunglasses to reveal dark blue and purple patches round and beneath her eyes. She walked straight to him and thrust her face close to his. Barely a half-inch separated them. He could feel a warmth from her skin. Skin that up close exposed a range of colours from the dark green of putrid meat to a bright yellow as though the skin held back a vat of puss waiting for a finger to probe and release it. All held together by red spidery veins.

'My stomach is much the same and I've got a nice large imprint of a shoe on my back.'

He could sense the anger inside her. Anger he knew was directed at him.

'But why?'

'Why? I've been pissing blood for nearly two days and you ask why. Why do you think?'

'I don't know.'

'Think, stupid.' Clara perched on the settee. Glaring at him. 'I didn't even know anything was wrong. One minute I'm standing in the kitchen making coffee, the next I'm on the floor with my eye swelling up. He didn't say a word of warning. I never even felt a thing, at least not with the first hit. But I felt the rest. Believe me, I felt the rest.'

Riley bent down on his knee next to her. 'You mean he knows?'

'Of course he knows Riley, you told him.'

Riley kept his face blank, as if he had no idea what she was talking about.

'Your phone call. Is Kathryn there?'

'You mean he guessed.'

'Guessed? Riley, he's not an idiot. That wouldn't fool a child.'

'I'm really sorry, Clara.'

He tried to take her hand, but she withdrew it from his grasp. Returning it to her pocket.

'What I don't understand is why you did it.' She looked at him pleadingly. 'Why?'

'I just phoned to talk to you. I needed someone to talk to.'

'And you never thought he'd answer the phone?'

'I never thought this would happen.'

'But you thought he might guess.'

'Does he know it's me?'

'Don't worry, he's not interested in who it is. I'm to blame, you see. I'm the one who gets punched.'

She got to her feet. Riley rose with her, unable to ignore the sense of relief he felt. He knew it was nearly over.

'I really didn't mean for this to happen, Clara.'

'No, you probably didn't. You had a laugh, though, didn't you? When you got off the phone. Making him suspicious. I bet you enjoyed it.' Tears squeezed their way past her heavily lined eyelashes. 'Just think, while you were giggling I was on the floor trying to cover myself.' She covered herself now, with the sunglasses. 'One day you'll wake up, Riley, and realize the sun doesn't shine out of your behind. I hurt. When he punched me, I hurt. Standing here now, I'm hurting. But you don't. You're not hurting at all.'

Riley followed her as she made her way out. She reached to unlock the front door but the door opened before she could touch it and revealed Sarah. Hand attached to the door by a key. Both women faced each other. Sarah wiggled the key free and stood aside. Clara walked out and down the stairs without a backward glance.

Riley went into the kitchen, filled the kettle, plugged it in and waited for it to boil. Sarah stood behind him.

'Where did you get the keys?'

'They were sitting in a bowl in the bedroom. I thought I'd surprise you.'

Riley rubbed his eyes, feeling weary. Listening to the roar of the kettle, which seemed to be out of proportion with the act of boiling water. It sounded more like he was standing at the base of Niagara Falls with the water pounding on his head. His fingers probed the soft flesh beneath his eyes and the ridge of his cheekbones. Seeking out relief until he had a flash of Clara's bruised face, then Nancy lying on black cloth. A line of stained cord striped across the photograph. He dropped his hand to the Formica surface the kettle sat on.

'Are you annoyed with me, Riley?'

'No. Do you want coffee?'

She slid her arms around his waist. Fingers interlocking at his midriff. 'Is that the last we'll see of her?'

'Yes, it is.' His body trembled. The waters of Niagara chilling him.

'What's wrong?'

'I did something bad.' She hugged him tighter. 'I pretended to myself that I didn't really mean it. I didn't know how bad it would be, but it's no excuse. No excuse at all.'

Sarah laid her head against his back. Her cheek pressed hard just below his shoulder blade. When she spoke, her words echoed through his chest. It felt to Riley that she was talking directly to his heart. 'As long as you know you've done something bad. Some people go through life without ever thinking about it.' She tugged at his elbow and he twisted round inside her arms to face her. 'Tell me it's different. That we're different.'

'We're different.'

She kissed him lightly. 'Now that you know it, I don't want you forgetting.'

He smiled. 'I won't. I've got a feeling you won't let me.'

'Don't worry. Every day I'll remind you how damn lucky you are to have me.'

The Truth

Light glowed from beyond the bamboo blind covering the window. Riley glanced at the time: 11.30. He got out of bed and opened the door of the built-in wardrobe. He fingered the cloth of his grey suit, but chose the dark blue one instead. Ties were always a problem. You very rarely came across a decent one. They were all spots or stripes or flowers in pastel shades. Worse still were the funny ones with go-go girls printed on them or the idiots who displayed Winnie-the-Pooh clutching a red balloon. He selected a plain gold tie. He draped it around the hanger for the suit and hung both on the handle of the wardrobe door. He padded through to the living room and unfolded the ironing board. He plugged in the iron, poured water through the hole in its top, then went back to the bedroom to fetch his shirt.

He'd already glided the iron across the back of the shirt and one sleeve when Sarah returned. Paper packages in hand.

'Croissants,' she said cheerily. 'What are you doing?'

'Work phoned. I've got to go in for a meeting.'

'On a Saturday?'

'Yeah. I'm afraid they do this every once in a while.'

Sarah opened one of the paper bags and dipped her nose into it. She sniffed the contents. 'Fresh pastry.' She said it with a disappointed tone.

'I've still got time for breakfast.' He dropped the iron and crossed the room to give her a reassuring hug. 'I'll whack some coffee on.'

'OK.'

She watched him busy about in the kitchen. 'What exactly is it you do anyway, Riley? We never did have that conversation.'

'The company I work for does financial tracking for other companies. Projections, company reports. I try to make the findings more interesting by writing them in an exciting manner. I suppose I'm a technical author. It's very boring. Not what I intended doing at all. I always wanted to write for the movies.'

'Why didn't you?'

Riley smiled at her. 'I never had any good ideas.'

'You should have stolen someone else's. That's what they do in the movies.'

'Yeah, I should have.'

'What time will you finish?'

'It'll probably go on all afternoon. I think I'll just go to my parents straight afterwards.'

'So I won't see you today?'

Riley carried the coffee into the living room. 'No, I don't think so.'

She pouted at him. 'I think you just don't want to know now you've had your way. Got what you want.'

He could see from the glint in her eye that she was teasing him, but he still felt uneasy. 'Don't be silly.'

'What about tomorrow?'

'I've got my daughter staying with me until Monday. You're more than welcome to join us, but it might not be your kind of thing. I don't know how you feel about children.'

Sarah looked bemused. 'I'm a woman. I know how I'm supposed to feel, but I haven't thought about it much.' She paused, closed her eyes, then snapped them open. 'Thought about it. I guess they're OK but maybe you'd like some time for her and yourself.'

'I'm not sure how much of that is sincere and how much is you ducking out.'

She grinned into her coffee. 'You'll never know.'

'Oh, I will. I intend to find out everything about you.'

'It's a lost cause, Riley. No one knows everything about anyone. We don't even know everything about ourselves.'

'Philosophy, eh?'

'Fact.'

He watched as she tore apart her croissant, dipping it into her coffee before lowering it into her mouth.

'What are you going to do today?'

'Oh, I'll just sit around on my own. Lonely. Be very, very bored.' Her face softened to the point of rupture, like a child who falls and slowly becomes aware of the impending pain. Expectant of an explosion of tears.

Riley could still see the glint in her eyes. 'Ha ha.'

Her smile returned. 'No, I think I'll probably go swimming. I fancy a dip in the pool. I haven't done it for a long time.'

'I could call you this evening. See how you are.'

Her smile broadened. 'Yes, well, I suppose bathing pools are dangerous and serious injury is a possibility.' She patted his knee. 'You better check on me, dear.'

'I'm only concerned.'

'I know.' She kissed him lightly. 'And I appreciate it.'

He drove through the city past the Saturday shoppers. The first wave of energy seeping from them. Leaving the bedraggled figures clinging to their shopping bags. A cup of coffee, a burger and they'd be off again to bruise the aisles of the department stores. He thanked God he was in his car going somewhere else. Anywhere else was preferable. He remembered his destination. Almost anywhere.

Saturday shopping had been another source of disappointment to Anne during their marriage. He tried to be interested. He really did. But fifteen minutes had been his limit. After that the pushing and shoving, the people lumbering along the streets at the speed of pregnant hippos, blocking the pavement, would become too much for him. He had to retire to the pub. Drink to soothe his nerves. His wife soon became a solo retail warrior. He didn't believe it was a gender thing. He knew other couples who did it. But he couldn't.

He got lucky and found a parking space waiting for him right outside Andrew's office. He opened the glove compartment and took out his twenty thousand pounds. The other ten lay stashed beneath his bed. Not the sort of hiding place to fool a burglar but everywhere else in the house seemed just as ludicrous. In the tea jar. Underneath the carpet. Behind a radiator or a bookcase. Looking back, he realized he could have left ten grand in the bank but he had withdrawn it all without thinking. Believing that this money was all he had as a saviour and he needed every penny in his hands.

The doorman didn't work weekends so he had to buzz Andrew's office to be let in.

'Hello?'

'It's me.'

'Come up.'

He pushed the door open and walked through the foyer, past the reception desk, and pressed the elevator button. The elevator announced its arrival with a swish of its parting doors. Riley entered and pressed for the seventh floor. As the doors closed, he thought how it was just another Saturday. Wake up with a new lover, bribe a government official, maybe pop to the pub to catch the football results and finally down to the prison for a state execution.

The door to the law firm's office was open. He went by Susan's empty desk and stepped into Andrew's room. The sight of the vacant leather chair threw him for a second until he realized Andrew was standing looking out of the window.

'Hi.'

'Hello.' Andrew returned his greeting without facing him.

Riley joined him at the window. 'What's happening?'

'Nothing much.' Andrew checked his watch. 'Our friend should be here any minute. Coffee?'

Riley nodded. 'I'm not sure my sphincter is up to it, but I'll force a cup down my throat.'

Andrew glanced at the package in Riley's hand. 'I take it that's the money?'

'Yeah.'

Andrew passed Riley the coffee. For the first time since Riley had entered the room, their eyes met. Andrew's gaze fell from Riley to the package.

'I did consider slipping the odd tenner out of the bundle, but decided against it.'

Andrew didn't smile at this feeble joke.

The office door opened and the contact stepped in. The sight of Mr Thompson in jeans and T-shirt, carrying a black Nike sports bag with some sort of racquet handle protruding, threw Riley slightly. It wasn't entirely unexpected and was the only equation that really made sense. Who else could it have been but James Thompson? The apparently wealthy civil servant in charge of the whole system.

Andrew broke the silence. 'I believe you two have already met.'

'Forgive me if I don't shake hands, James.'

James Thompson smiled in an easy, relaxed manner. 'Of course I'll forgive you.' He eased himself into the chair behind Andrew's desk and rested his bag on the floor. A moment passed after Riley and Andrew sat down. James cleared his throat. 'Shall we get down to business?' James's eyes settled on Riley's coffee cup. 'You couldn't fetch me a cup of coffee, could you, Andrew?'

Andrew rose to get the coffee. As he did so, Riley put the package on the desk.

James looked at the package but didn't touch. Instead he accepted the coffee and sipped from his cup.

'It's all there,' Riley said.

'Of course it is, Riley.' James allowed a small hint of satisfaction to creep into his smile. 'I never doubted it would be.'

'So what's the deal? Can I go home now or do I still have to go to the prison?'

Andrew's silence was unsettling Riley. Why was his lawyer suddenly struck mute?

James nodded, as if contemplating a serious question. 'The deal.' Suddenly his hint of satisfaction split into a large grin. 'The strange thing is, Riley, I'm afraid I'm not going to be able to take your money.'

Riley leaned across the desk and pushed the package towards James. 'But it's all there. As we agreed.'

'I know, you said that.'

'Then what the fuck is going on?' His brain hadn't got far enough to search into the implications of this turn of events, but Andrew's visible lack of surprise sent a rattle of panic through his nervous system like a freight train thundering through deserted stations in the middle of the night. After the noise only a chill and an unnatural stillness were left behind. 'You knew this, didn't you?'

The question, asked quietly, required no answer. Andrew's steady look said it all.

'Why? Why lead me to believe this was going to work out?'

James sipped his coffee. 'It's a question that deserves an answer. He did so because I asked him to. That's what people in our business do, ask favours.'

'So, why ask him?'

'Because I wanted you to believe you could buy your way out.'

'But you never had any intentions of taking it.'

'No. I'm not deriding your means, but to take your money would be like breaking into the Bank of England, stealing the cashbox and ignoring the safe. Do you realize how much money there is in the death penalty? How much it actually costs to kill a man, or, more to the point, how much you can charge?'

'No.'

'Millions. And it's a growth industry. I'm not advocating through greed that anyone enjoys the trip at the end of a rope regardless of guilt or innocence, but there are enough people out there deserving of it. And, more importantly, it's what the public want. Revenge. Justice seen to be done, or at least they can read in the morning paper about justice being done. It makes them feel that bit better about life as they set off to work. One less killer on the streets. You see, Riley, there are aspects to this you don't seem to understand. One is that the Addison Corporation, who run our prison service, just can't make a big enough profit out of locking people up. They can cut staff and pay them peanuts. They can run down their facilities, feed the prisoners less well, but the numbers will never add up. The execution side of the business brings in valuable revenue that can be used to compensate for less profitable areas of the company. Effectively it means we have better, safer, more secure prisons. Therefore better, safer, more secure streets.'

'That's all very well and noble, but what has that to do with me. It still doesn't matter who helps out to finish off Hughes. It doesn't explain why you won't take the money. And why do you care about the Addison Corporation's profit margin? You're a civil servant.'

'I am a civil servant, but I won't always be. You see, I designed the system that is now being used for executions.'

Riley felt himself slipping back into the worn leather of the chair. 'What did you design?'

'It's all very simple. The Addison Corporation always knew that executions could bolster their profit margin and were very keen to get it back on the agenda. There was never any chance, though. No government was ever going to even entertain the idea. Any restoration of the death penalty would contravene the European Convention on Human Rights, for God's sake. But Europe is weak. Anyone can override it. The main obstacle was the politicians. Addison knew the public were all for it. Year in, year out, private polls showed a massive majority in favour. The government knew that as well, that's why they fought so hard not to even have a debate about it. Because once public opinion is let loose then the politicians have to follow. That's the beauty of democracy.

'Maybe nothing would have happened if it hadn't been for Mr Henderson. You remember Mr Henderson, don't you?'

'Yeah.'

Riley remembered him all too well. Near the end of his hunger strike his weak, emaciated figure being carried triumphantly from the street outside the Home Office as the government backed down and agreed to debate the death penalty. Hands in the air, like a striker who bangs in the winner in the last minute of extra time. 'This is a victory for justice and the victims of crime,' he had said into the glaring lights of the cameras.

'It scared the shit out of them, his hunger strike. Then there was the street demonstrations. You can't ignore a hundred thousand people marching along the streets of London or the thousands in Glasgow, Leeds, Manchester, Birmingham. All over. You can't ignore that if you're a minority government in coalition. Especially when the media supports the return of the death penalty and the opposition do a U-turn and decide they too support stringing up the villains of the day. The pressure is unstoppable. Still the government held out, and that's where I came in.'

'You had the big idea?'

James grinned at Riley. 'You've guessed. It was my idea to have the government announce the referendum with the proviso that those who voted yes would have to actively take part. It was a piece of genius. I mean, who would ever have believed that, faced with a choice like that, people would actually vote for it? It was inconceivable. The government could give the go-ahead for a referendum safe in the knowledge that it would fail and that would be the end of the matter.'

'But you knew it would pass.'

James shrugged. 'I didn't know for sure. It was a gamble I had to persuade Addison and others to take. My reasoning was that people generally don't really think things through much. That they tend to respond with their guts and their guts would say two things. One, yeah, let's get rid of all the paedophiles and rapists and murderers. The world will be a better place. And secondly, rather perversely if you think about it, that it wouldn't be them called in to do the dirty deed. What were the odds in that?' James started to laugh. 'It's strange if you think how many people actually buy a lottery ticket every fucking week with exactly the opposite reasoning. That it will be them.'

'Fuck.'

'Don't tell me that's how your brain filtered it all out, Riley?'

'I don't play the lottery, but I can't say that it got much more philosophical than that.' Riley picked up his cold coffee and swirled the dregs around the bottom of the cup. 'So when you leave the civil service, the Addison Corporation might just have an opening suitable for you.'

'I think they will. An extremely lucrative opening that I don't really have to do very much to fill.'

'But you don't want to be tainted with a bribe?'

James Thompson flicked an invisible speck of dirt from the

front of his sparkling white T-shirt. 'Are you hinting at the irony in the situation?'

'Just a little. I don't see what all this has to do with me. Why me? We're all friends here. Favours is what you said made the world go round.'

'True, it does, but you're not in the club. I'm already doing someone a favour. And anyway, there are so many reasons why it is you. From an altruistic point of view you were chosen. Why should someone else be put in the shit just because you've changed your mind? You voted yes. You put yourself here.'

'But it still might not be me. It might be one of the others.'

'True. So take your chances.'

'All I'm asking is you shorten the odds for the other two by taking my name off the list.'

James rose from his seat. 'No. Like I said, I'm already doing someone a favour. That's why you're on the list.'

Riley couldn't understand what James was saying. 'Do you mean someone asked you to put me on the list? Who?'

'I'm afraid you'll have to sort this out with your lawyer.'

Andrew remained mute. His face impassive. Eyes staring blindly into Riley's face.

James checked his watch. 'Right, I've got to go. Squash in half an hour.' He grabbed his bag, hoisted it over his shoulder and made for the door. 'There is a car waiting downstairs to escort you to the prison, Riley. Make sure you are there for 5, otherwise you will find your stay extended for a very long time.' James paused in the doorway. 'You know, in some ways I envy you. It's going to be a very interesting experience. Goodbye.'

The door closed with a quiet click of the lock.

Riley's legs struggled to find the energy to lift him out of his chair. He wandered across the room to the window and leaned heavily against its frame. He wondered if this was what it felt like to drown in extremely cold water. He'd read somewhere that the longest you could survive in the choppy waters of the North Sea was around ten minutes. This last week felt like his ten minutes. The initial shock and now the intensifying numbness. His senses slowly shutting down. The loss of feeling in his fingers and his toes. The sensation spreading through his limbs until he was aware of only his heart and the blood it pumped through his collapsing system. The heat from the blood dissipating on its journey until it solidified and its pathway became blocked. His veins and arteries hardening. Is this what it felt like to drown?

Outside, the sun had appeared with a late-autumn golden shine. The sky held a tinge of red in its thin streak of clouds. Pigeons followed each other along the ledge of the building facing him. The girl he had watched the other day was gone and in her place sat a man. Short fair hair. Headset on. White shirt and tie. Craning towards a computer screen. Hands flitting over the keyboard. Sorting out someone's problems.

Andrew handed Riley another cup of coffee. He knew the liquid was scalding his lips but couldn't feel the results. It didn't revive him.

'So you knew he wasn't going to take the money?'

'Yes, I knew.'

'Is it you he's doing the favour for?'

'It's me.'

The cold seeped through his veins, reaching the ventricles of his heart. He reached out and touched the soft pink skin of his friend's face. 'Why?'

'It's hard to explain.'

'I'd like you to try. It's kinda important, Andrew.'

'It's because you voted yes. You voted to kill people.'

'So did millions of others.'

'You don't understand.'

'No, I obviously fucking don't,' Riley snapped. 'I don't

understand at all.' The final ounce of energy left his body. He dropped his cup and staggered to sit down like a man hit by sniper fire. The coffee sprayed black across the grey wool carpet. 'Why don't you enlighten me, Andrew?'

Andrew took a chair opposite. 'Do you remember how we met?'

'Of course I remember.'

'Tell me about it then.'

'Why do I need to tell you about it? You were there.'

'Just tell me,' Andrew pleaded.

'I was coming home through the park pissed. I heard you shouting and I found you being robbed by some guy with a knife. I chased him off and we've been friends ever since. There.'

'And what was I doing in the park?'

'You'd gone to get some chocolate from the garage. You'd been studying late.'

'And you believed that?'

'What the fuck is this? Cross-examination?'

'I'm asking if that's what you believe. If you still believe that.'

'Yes.'

'Do you?'

'Yes.'

'Why didn't I get chocolate from a machine in the halls?'

'I don't fucking know. Maybe they were out. Maybe you didn't have any change. Maybe you fancied a walk.'

'Maybe I was going to the park to find someone to have sex with. Maybe I'd heard it was a cruising spot.'

Riley couldn't respond. He could see tears hanging on the precipice of the corners of Andrew's eyes. It wasn't that Riley hadn't thought about this before. It was just he'd always pushed those thoughts away.

'Look at me, Riley. Look at what I am.'

'I didn't vote to kill gay people, Andrew. I don't care if you're gay.'

Was that true? If so, why had he always stopped himself thinking about it?

'No, you're not looking properly. Look at me.'

Riley examined the rounded features, a boy's face still waiting to be a man. The thin wisps of fair hair struggling strenuously to be sideburns. Eyelashes that were long and graceful in their curve. Girls would die for eyelashes like Andrew's.

'I'll tell you what I am. I'm a fucking freak. I've been a freak ever since I can remember. I'm not talking about the child-genius shit. Although none of that helped. All the crap about being an expert mathematician at seven and speaking five languages at ten. All that did was make me stand out, and I didn't want to stand out. I wanted to be like everybody else. When I was fourteen, just before going to university, I lost my virginity. I had sex with a thirteen-year-old boy at school called Steven. And that's where I've been ever since. I'm stuck. I've tried everything. I've buried myself in law, which is a touch ironic. I've taken on all the trappings of a man. I smoke cigars. I hate cigars and yet I smoke four or five a day. Even at home on my own, as if I have to try and fool myself. I play golf. I play football. But this sickness is inside me. I try hard to fight it, but it's too bloody strong. I get tired. It always wins. I fuck women. I fuck men. It doesn't work. It just makes it worse. Eventually I have to go away. I have to give in.'

'Like your recent trip to Stuttgart?'

Andrew smiled a weak smile. 'No, that was an excuse to avoid you.' Riley returned the smile. 'But you do get it, Riley? You do get what I am saying?'

Riley nodded yes.

Andrew leaned forward and clasped Riley's hands. 'I need to say it. I need to be sure.'

'Don't.'

'I have to. I like having sex with young boys.'

Riley broke free from his hands. He got up and strode back to the window. Leaning his forehead against the cold hard surface of the glass. The sun had dipped quickly. He saw Andrew approaching. His reflection almost obliterated by the searing orange of the streetlights.

'I never wanted to tell you. I knew it would be the end for us. I find it hard enough to live with myself. How could I expect anyone else to even come close to understanding? But that's the difference, Riley. The world is made for people like you. Male white heterosexuals. You waltz through life. I'll never have that. I'll never be accepted. I'll always be vilified. Despised. But at least I could hide. Pretend. Even pretending that if you ever did know you would somehow understand or at least try to. My best friend. But there you were in the pub, full of lager and hate. Singing along with everyone else. No different. No better. I couldn't pretend any more. You were voting to kill me.'

'I didn't know that.'

Andrew laid a hand on his shoulder. 'I don't think it would have made any difference. It doesn't, does it?'

'I don't know Andrew.' The hand slipped from his shoulder. 'I take it my inclusion in the Hughes's hanging wasn't really a quirk of the electoral roll?'

'No, it wasn't.'

'Your way of teaching me a lesson.'

'I wanted you to know what you had done.' Andrew returned to his chair behind the large oak desk. He switched on a lamp and illuminated the office that had dipped into late-afternoon winter gloom.

Riley retrieved his coffee cup from the floor and placed it on a tray next to the coffee machine. He drifted over to the desk and picked up his money. He looked at his friend sitting in his oversized leather chair, doodling on a notepad with his Mont Blanc fountain pen.

'I take it for your plan to be entirely successful I would have to be the candidate chosen?'

'You are the only candidate Riley. There are no others.'

Riley turned his back and started to walk. He paused at the door, searching for something to say, but he couldn't make sense of his thoughts. He closed the door quietly behind him. Listening to the hum of the strip-lighting, he waited in the hall, but didn't know what he was waiting for. Andrew to come and get him? Breakdown? But who was Andrew? He realized he didn't know. He left.

Still the heavens refused to open and bless the city with anything more than a fine spray of drizzle. The car was cold and Riley got the heater blasting to try and warm himself. The street, lined by offices, was empty.

'I like to have sex with young boys.' How young? Where did he meet them?

The air from the heater seemed to roll over him. It reacted badly with the cold air in his lungs and his stomach contracted. He tried breathing slowly, but couldn't regain control and was hit by another spasm. He opened the car door and puked on to the pavement. Watery dark liquid with an acidic taste. It left an ugly film on his throat and teeth. He tried rinsing his mouth with spit. The rain on the back of his neck soothed him. He righted himself and clutched hard on the steering wheel, as if he'd just hit a bend too quickly and had to struggle to regain control of the car.

How young were the boys?

Eventually he managed to close the door, but as soon as he'd done so someone tapped on the window. He lowered the glass and faced a middle-aged man with short grey hair and dark brown eyes. A colour that reminded Riley of the liquid that had recently left his body.

'Are you all right, sir?' the man asked.

'What's it to you?'

'I'm your escort to the prison.'

'Oh, I see. I'm fine. Too much coffee on an empty belly.'

'Right, as long as you are OK. I'm right behind you sir, so I'll pull out and if you want to follow me, we'll get there in no time at all.'

'It's a bit early, isn't it? I'm due there at five.'

'Unless there's somewhere else you want to go before.'

'No.'

'You're sure you can drive? You can always come in my car or I can hang on a minute or two, let you get your breath.'

'No, I'm fine. Let's go.' Riley turned the ignition key and revved the engine into life. The prison didn't seem like such a scary place to go after all.

Lights were low as Riley entered the cell. He could make out the figure of Hughes in his blue overalls on a bed in the corner. Back to the room. His legs drawn to his chest and his hands hugging his knees. Riley plumped himself down on one of the two wooden chairs arranged round a small wooden table at the other side of the cell. The air in the room was terrible. Stale sweat and a scent of oil that seemed to permeate every place on the ship.

He studied the chess game laid out on the table. White was already two pawns down and its queen looked vulnerable. A high-class girl who had strayed into the wrong kind of bar. She now stood exposed, out front on the wings. Waiting to be boxed in. Captured. Black had castled and its pawns forged through the middle of the board in a menacing V formation.

Riley didn't know a lot about chess but he knew that white should be the dominant force and was in for a very rough ride in this game. What had happened to white? He pondered a few moves to try and rescue the queen, but became bored with the possibilities. Instead he unfolded the broadsheet lying on the other chair and tried to get interested in the lead story about the London mayor being prosecuted for fraud. Two hundred thousand missing and a paper trail to an offshore account. Construction contracts given to certain select companies. Why would anyone be surprised at shit like that? Riley wondered.

Hughes stared out at him in the form of a grainy black and white photograph in the bottom right-hand corner of the front page. The article just churned out the basic facts. Killer of Nancy to die. Only possibility an intervention by the Home Secretary.

'Are you reading anything interesting?'

Riley lowered the paper. Hughes faced him, eyes sparkling through the dim light. 'No. Just the usual rubbish that fills a paper.'

Hughes hauled himself into a sitting position, rubbing at his face with his hands. A book fell from his lap to the floor. He bent to retrieve it.

'What about you? Reading anything interesting?'

'*In Cold Blood* by Truman Capote. Have you heard of it?'

'Yes.'

'Unfortunately, I've just started it. I don't suppose you know how it ends?'

'Are you being smart?'

Hughes grinned, exposing teeth like slabs of marble. 'Just a little bit.' He took the other chair. 'I told you we'd meet again.'

The thought made Riley laugh. 'Yeah, I think you knew a lot more than I did.'

'I'm looking forward to having a chat with you during dinner. You will join me for dinner?'

'How could I resist? Of course I will.'

'Good.' Hughes rubbed some more at his eyes, then moved a pawn forward in support of the queen.

'Who were you playing?'

Two lines ran down the side of Hughes's face where he had been lying. He traced their path with his forefinger. 'One of the guards. I was black, but I don't mind taking the other side.'

Before Riley could respond to the move, the cell flashed into brightness and the door was unlocked. Hughes checked his watch, then stood up.

'I've got to go. I have to say farewell to Sylvia, my wife.'

Riley followed him to the door and tugged on the sleeve of one of the guards.

'What?'

'Is there a telephone I can use? It's for a private call.'

'Sure. Just let me get him settled and then I'll come back for you.'

The telephone was answered after three rings.

'Hello?'

'Hello, Sarah, it's me.'

'Hello, me, it's great to hear your voice. I've been thinking quite a bit about you today.'

'Have you?'

'There's no need to sound so surprised.'

'I'm not. Well, maybe just a little bit. What kind of day have you had?'

'It's been good actually. I went to the pool and stayed in the water so long that I came out looking like a prune. A slender and shapely prune, but still a prune. It was quite freakish in a way, 'cause it gave me an idea of what I might look like in forty years' time. I was relieved you weren't there. Anyway, then I had some lunch, then I bought an absolutely drop dead gorgeous dress with my credit card which I love but will regret when the bill comes in and then I went home. What about your day?'

'Very long and very boring.'

'Was your meeting OK?'

'The results weren't what I hoped for, but I'll survive.'

'Good. Are you at your parents'?'

'No, not yet. The meeting went on for a while. I'm on my way there now. I'm calling from a service station.'

'Oh.' She sounded worried. 'Didn't want to phone in front of Mum and Dad, eh? Doesn't want them to know about the latest floozy.'

'No, no, no. I just thought I'd better ring now in case you were going out later.'

'Good guess. I am about to hop in the bath before hitting the town tonight. I'm having a drink with some friends.'

'OK. I'll let you get on. I was thinking maybe we could go out Monday night. You could wear your new dress.'

'It'll have to be somewhere expensive Riley, to befit the dress.'

'Trying to manoeuvre me into expensive restaurants already. OK, you win, expensive it is.'

'Call me at work on Monday then.'

'OK. And Sarah, some people might say that it is a touch early in our relationship, but I love you.'

Her words came to him in a steady, measured tone. 'I wouldn't say it was too early. I love you too. Bye.'

The Sunday

'I hope you're not a vegetarian.'

'Why?' Riley asked. 'What's on the menu?'

'Meat and lots of it.' Hughes read from a card taken from his overall pocket. 'Wild mushroom and chicken boudin blanc, followed by lamb cutlets with savoy cabbage and rounded off with the classic tiramisu and home-made chocolate ice cream. They're bringing a chef across the water specially to prepare the meal.'

'Wow.'

They fell into concentrated eating when the first course arrived and only managed the odd sentence throughout. Riley, with his sides aching, eventually dropped his spoon and flopped back in his chair with exhaustion. He hadn't really eaten properly for days and struggled with the quality of the meal.

'That was bloody good.'

'Yeah, it was. Not like the shit they serve you every day in this toilet. Unfortunately, no wine. It must be bad manners to arrive at your own neck-tie party the worse for wear.'

'I don't know what I expected, but I think it was more in the order of fried shrimp, crayfish or lobster. Every time I've seen something on the death penalty on TV that's the kind of stuff they've always had for their last meal. Heavy seafood.'

'That's the States. All them good 'ole southern boys. At least you have to say that the proportion of white people executed to black in Britain is far superior to America. We're 100 per cent Caucasian at the moment.' Hughes laid his dessert spoon to rest. 'Do you think I deserve to die, Riley?'

Riley toyed with his final spoonful of tiramisu. Trying to decide whether it would make him sick or not. 'I don't know. I don't know if you intended to kill her. I don't know if you'd do it again.'

'Is that what matters? Isn't Nancy enough?'

Riley saw Nancy. The bruised and battered face laid out against the black cloth. The thin deep cut the cord had made around her throat. The blood rushing to the wound like a frozen waterfall caught in the act of tipping over the precipice.

'Why did you say she was a prostitute?'

Hughes lowered his head to his hands. He shivered despite the warmth in the cell. When he raised his eyes Riley detected the first sign of a crack behind them. A glimpse of what was falling apart inside.

'When I visited Sylvia tonight, Riley, that's when I really felt bad. She's a good woman. I know that's a stock phrase, but there is no other way to describe her. She doesn't deserve any of this. She doesn't deserve the pain or misery that a large chunk of the rest of her life will be. Perhaps this will haunt her to the day she dies. She'll have to move. She's been getting all the usual threats people in her position get. Standard stuff. Hate mail, anonymous phone calls, abuse in the street. She makes light of it, but she's aged badly since all this began. She hasn't said, but I know friends are scarce on the ground. Dinner party invitations tend to dwindle when your husband's been convicted of murder. It's not like she's even got financial security for comfort. The house won't be easy to sell and my insurance company have a whole legal squad poring over my policies, trying to discover a way to default on payment when I'm gone. It's a tricky one. Apparently the government and the insurance firms didn't bother to figure it out before jumping on to the execution bandwagon. My lawyers are hopeful, but it could take a few years to come through.

'My one hope is that she'll move on some day, in a real sense. Maybe meet someone else. Someone to make her happy. Make her laugh again. You're asking me why I lied. I did it for Sylvia. When the police came round the first time she was furious. Furious that they would even think to question me. I was clean, Riley. The worst I'd ever had was a parking ticket. The only time I ever broke the law was at university, when I'd dabbled with the odd acid trip or joint, but I wasn't exactly in the minority there. I'm sure you can vouch for that. She believed in me, you see, even as the evidence mounted, even when my lawyers told her there was no hope, that my story wouldn't fool a child.

'I didn't want to appeal, but I knew that I had to. I wanted it over with, but if I'd told Sylvia the truth it would have destroyed her. So I kept going. In all the months since I was taken into custody, she has never once questioned me or castigated me about having sex with Nancy. Not once. I felt I had to give her reasons as to why it happened. A half-naked, half-drunk little whore who lured me when I wasn't well.'

'Does she still believe you didn't kill her?'

'I'm sure that deep down she knows I did it, but she can give reasons now as to why. It is easier for her to see a weak fool who panicked when things went too far. Who never really intended any harm. She can relate that to the man she spent twenty-three years of her life with. I've pondered this a lot in my cell. Whether it is worse to destroy someone's future or to destroy someone's past. To make a mockery of what their life has been about. I still haven't came to a satisfactory answer. All I know is that Sylvia doesn't have to pass each minute of the day thinking that her partner was a rapist and a murderer.'

'And that is what you are?'

'Yes. Without a doubt. You can rest easy tomorrow. You won't be carrying out a miscarriage of justice. Will you rest easy?'

Riley pushed his chair back from the table and stretched his legs. 'That's another "don't know" from me. All I've done this week is try everything to have someone else sitting in this chair besides myself.'

'It was all a waste of time, wasn't it?'

'A complete waste of time. How did you know it was me when we met in the canteen?'

'I told you, I saw you in the future.'

Riley couldn't keep the smile of disbelief off his face. 'That's bullshit.'

'You think so? I asked you if I deserved to die. I'll answer the question for you. I voted for the death penalty. So I knew what to expect. It didn't stop me. Nothing would have stopped me. But afterwards I understood the consequences of what I had done. The moral question of whether a society has the right to extinguish its own citizens is a highly debatable one, but we had the debate and we still went ahead. You went ahead. Just like me. You wonder if I meant to kill her. When I was lying in bed, in the dark, soaked in fever for weeks afterwards, I pretended that I hadn't, but the truth is I made the decision as soon as I opened my front door to find her standing on the steps.'

'She came to your house?'

'Yes. Somehow she knew that Sylvia wasn't going to be around. God knows how. I still haven't been able to figure that one out. Normally Sylvia and I spent Saturdays together, doing what couples do, but her mother was ill.' Hughes closed his eyes and gently rubbed at his temples with his forefingers. 'I had this feeling. An odd out-of-sorts feeling. I put it down to the cold or flu or whatever the hell I had, but maybe the anxiousness I felt in my chest, the tightness, was more of a premonition. It's like when you've been drinking heavily and the next day every time the phone rings you think it's going to be bad news. Except I hadn't been drinking. I tried to shake it off, but by the time I dropped Sylvia at her mum's I almost asked her to come back with me. Instead I waved her goodbye. When I got to the house it only intensified. I drank a large Scotch and failed to lose myself in a rugby match on TV. When the doorbell rang I almost banged my head on the ceiling I was so wound up. I don't know whether my senses were heightened, but I could actually smell her perfume filtering through the door. Can you believe that? So I wasn't surprised when I opened it to find her standing there. She was the only person I knew who wore it. I don't know the name. It's quite a delicate, understated fragrance. There was nothing understated about the huge fucking smile she gave me, along with a chirpy "Hi" and the lame excuse of being in the neighbourhood. If I hadn't been in a fever before I certainly was then.' Hughes opened his eyes. 'You've seen pictures of Nancy?'

'Yes.'

'Pictures don't do her justice.' The lids of his eyes lowered again until they were firmly shut. 'We had history, you see, Riley. Not an affair or anything like that. It's trite and I wouldn't say it to her mother, but I did care for her. I cared a lot.

'A year or two before on a school trip to France I found her crying in one of the rooms. Everyone else had gone off on a visit to Versailles for the day, so we were the only ones around. She told me she'd got drunk and slept with one of the boys and how he was bragging about it to anyone who would listen.

'We had a good day that day. We were staying at one of the

universities. I forget the name now, but they rent rooms and dorms during the summer. The campus was quite spread out and a lot of the buildings were surrounded by garden. It was really hot and sunny. We just walked around and talked a lot. We even had some dinner in a café together and a couple of glasses of wine. It was just like two people enjoying being together, not like teacher and pupil. We did kiss, which scared the hell out of me, but Nancy was actually pretty mature about it. She gave me a lot of reassurance that it wouldn't go any further, that no one would know. And that was that. Our relationship didn't progress any. At school she was just another pupil, neither of us mentioned France and then she moved on.' Hughes paused. He glanced at Riley expectantly.

'What?'

'I thought you were going to dispute that point.'

'Why would I dispute it?'

'Because it sounds implausible. That there weren't any repercussions. Well, there weren't, at least nothing obvious, but France had created a bond between us. At first I put what had happened down to the lure of Paris, but every time I saw her I felt it. A craving. Months would pass and I would bump into her in the street and it always felt stronger. The traffic, people pushing past me, the noise, it all disappeared. The craving never diminished. No wonder addicts find it so hard to give up. She felt it too, you know, the excitement, the rush of energy, but she misinterpreted it. She thought we were going to be lovers. If that was what we were going to amount to, it would have happened sooner, probably on that first day in France, but I held off because I was scared, Riley. Not of discovery but because of what was inside me. I was a killer.'

Hughes hunched forward, his chin close to the surface of the table. Riley had to lean in to catch his words. He noticed the sweat glistening on Hughes's skin, sparkling beneath the harsh lighting like a galaxy of tiny stars.

'We know there are two worlds, don't we, Riley? The everyday, run-of-the-mill existence and the other world. The one that centres around ourselves. It's a delicate balancing act how much we let one invade the other. Sometimes we get it wrong. Like with Clara.'

Riley tried hard not to take the bait but couldn't help himself. 'How do you know about Clara?'

'You got a file on me, Riley... well, on the case. I got a file on you.'

Nerves crept into Riley's voice. 'Me?'

'Yes, you. I can't believe this is any shock. Didn't you think the government would bother with someone like you? They keep files on almost everyone, Riley. I'm privy to this information since I shan't be spreading it too far.'

'So they're watching me?' Riley attempted a jokey tone but failed.

'Of course they are. Do you feel bad about Clara? The beating she took.'

'It wasn't my fault.'

'Wasn't it? You called her husband. You don't carry any responsibility? Any shame or guilt? Have you even thought about her since?'

'I know I made a mistake by calling but –'

'But,' Hughes cut in. 'I've been waiting for the but. The truth is, you made a deliberate mistake.'

'I didn't mean for her to get hurt. I didn't think through what would happen. How was I to know her husband beat her?'

'Is that the mental process you brought to bear when you cheated on your wife? I said to you earlier that I couldn't decide whether it was worse to destroy someone's future or their past. Can you tell me? How did it feel to destroy your wife's past? Take away her self-esteem, her dignity?'

'Fuck you, Hughes. Lots of people cheat on their partners. I'm not a fucking saint.'

'That doesn't make it right.'

'No, it doesn't, but neither is it a capital crime, as you should know.'

'True, but you still hurt someone, destroyed a part of them. And what about your little redhead? The one you fucked the other night. Her name is April, in case you're interested. She trotted off to the family planning clinic the next morning for a pill. They're not particularly nice, those pills. She spent the rest of the day in bed throwing up into a bucket.'

Riley fiddled with one of the chess pieces. A white bishop. 'I made a mistake.'

'I made a mistake too. A deliberate mistake.'

'I'm not a murderer.'

'No, men like you aren't murderers. You still get a thrill, though, don't you, Riley? You get a thrill thinking about being in bed with her. Fucking her. About doing the wrong thing.' Hughes reached and took hold of Riley's hand. 'You questioned whether I would do it again and right now, in a lucid sensible moment, I'd say no, but we all say that. Whether it's sitting with a hangover or when we've made a tit of ourselves, in that period of vulnerability we all say never again. But I know I would. I spent years building up to it. In my mind I'd done it to hundreds of girls before, Nancy included. It was my little kick. What do you fantasize about, Riley? I fantasize about hurting people. About tying girls up, holding them down, forcing them to do things.'

'Raping them.'

'No, not in my head. In my head they say no, they fight and struggle, but in the end they've come round. They enjoy it.'

'Not Nancy?'

'No. Not Nancy. I'd gone through scenarios for years. How these situations would occur. Not one of them started with the girl knocking on my door. It all clicked into place, seeing her standing in her short black skirt, black knee-length boots and this really tight low-cut silver top. I invited her in for a drink, and as much as I'd made my decision, I'm pretty sure she'd made hers too. She was flirting with me. Blatantly. And we kissed for a while. I made an excuse that I felt uncomfortable being in the house. The presence of Sylvia and rubbish of that sort. It's one of the reasons I know that I fully intended to kill her. Nothing would have happened in the house. She was safe there. I'd only have cheated on my wife for the first time since we'd exchanged our vows.

'When we got to the woods the kissing and fondling started all over again, until someone drove into the car park beside us. It was a pretty silly place for us to be doing that and I was annoyed about it, but Nancy thought it was really funny. She kept laughing. My temperature was going through the roof. We had a few pulls on a hip flask I'd brought. I'm not a heavy drinker or anything, I take it when I go hill walking in the summer. We walked into the woods. It was a beautiful day. The sun hung on the horizon like molten gold. It couldn't have been that much colder under the trees, but it felt like you'd stepped into winter. My body seemed to have taken in the heat of the sun. I mean that literally. Every muscle, every sinew, my skin had caught fire. We had sex and I must have been a bit rough with her even then, because after it she was quiet, really quiet. I still had her in my arms. I still lay on top of her, our faces were no distance apart, and I saw the fear in her eyes. It reminded me of all those fantasies. That look. That was how it always started. It turned me on like nothing else. I lost control completely.'

Hughes remained quiet for a long time. His eyes fused with memory. A junkie who's just had a very strong hit. His hand still grasped Riley, who sat trying not to move, not to breathe, not to break the spell. When speech returned to Hughes, his words came slowly, thick and slurred.

'Young girls are hungry, Riley. Hungry to be women. That's

what makes them vulnerable. I can't lie to you. There is no point. It was great. It was better than I had ever imagined. I felt reborn. Nothing can ever replace it. I can't turn back. Lying in my sickbed in the weeks after, I thought of her. Every movement, every gesture, every expression. I almost fooled myself that I had created it all in my mind as usual.' Hughes slipped his hand away from Riley and folded his arms. He rested his head on them. 'I couldn't escape the truth though. You see, when it was over and Nancy had died, I felt a lot of tenderness towards her. I told you earlier that I cared for her and I did. I kissed her goodbye. A long, drawn-out kiss. A lovers' kiss. I hadn't reckoned, though, on death being there, on death being trapped alongside her last breath. Ever since that kiss I've had corpses in my mouth. I can taste nothing else except her. It's not guilt, Riley, it's truth.' Hughes's voice faded to a whisper. 'I'm tired now. I'm going to sleep. Not what you're supposed to do with your final hours, I suppose, but it's what I want to do. Be careful, Riley. It's dangerous to try and make your dreams into reality. Keep them to yourself. Keep them as dreams.'

Riley gathered the white pieces and arranged them along their two rows on the board, then did the same with the black. He went through a few opening moves before returning the pieces to their original positions. He fought against his own eyes, which were heavy with sleep. A vague thought crossed his mind that the food had been drugged to keep them both quiet.

Startling summer sunshine blinded him. A black figure swung into his face, making him duck, then swung away again. He squinted against the light and managed to make out the figure of a child in a swing. Tiny fingers clinging to the chains. The child swung high into the distance, then came back to him with a rush of wind. His daughter was grinning. Her long brown hair trailing after her. She was much younger than now and wore a vivid green dress he recognized and a pair of red wellington boots that she had insisted on wearing every day for the length of an entire summer, despite the lack of rain. His hands reached out and pushed her higher. There was no dialogue between them, just the endless rhythmical swinging of her in and out of his sight.

When he woke, Hughes had gone. He squirmed out of his slumped position in the chair and massaged the stiffness from his neck. A guard stood by the doorway. Riley recognized him as the one Lewis had called Simon.

'Where's the prisoner?'

Simon chewed on some gum thoughtfully. 'Getting changed. There's some tea in the urn on the trolley. It might help you freshen up.'

Riley poured some tea into a polystyrene cup and added a drop of milk. 'How are things with the general population out there?'

'Quiet.'

'I thought Mr Lewis said it all got a bit wild in here during an execution.'

'That's something I've got to look forward to.' He tugged on his thick black belt. His short wooden stick swinging by his side, tapping his thigh. 'The riot boys are on call, but any mayhem won't start until the hanging is over. Before, everything dies down. An expectancy descends on the place. It reminds me of some old horror film where everybody in the village cowers behind their doors because it's the day of the month when the monster who lives in the woods comes out to eat one of them.'

'We're the monsters then?'

'Yes, we are.'

The cell door opened and Hughes entered, followed by another guard. His blue overalls had been replaced with freshly laundered brilliant white ones.

Riley smiled at him. 'Very nice.'

Hughes returned the smile. 'Yes, very dapper, aren't they?' He raised his hands in front of his face to display the handcuffs binding them together. 'I've been made safe now. My electronic band is off and we've gone for the more traditional method of control.'

'Would you like some tea?'

'How civilized. Yes please, milk no sugar.'

Riley passed him a cup. Hughes lowered himself on to the edge of his bed and sipped at his tea. 'What time is it?'

The question was asked to the room in general. Simon spoke first. '4.50.'

'Not long now.'

Riley's hands trembled as he lifted his own cup. He leaned back against the wall to steady himself. Afraid his legs might give way. 'No, not long.'

The words had barely escaped his lips before the cell door opened. A short balding man in a grey double-breasted suit stood in the doorway. He was followed in by the stocky figure of Johnson, who also sported a double-breasted suit but in a dark blue wool. The man in grey laid a hand on the shoulder of the prisoner.

'All ready, Tim?' He spoke with a thin watery lisp that matched his large blue eyes, which seemed to be on the verge of tears.

'Yes, sir.'

'How are you feeling?'

'I'll be fine.'

'Good.' The man took a folded sheet of paper from his coat pocket. 'I'm sorry but I have to carry out the formalities and read out the conviction and sentence, OK?'

'Go ahead.'

The man unfolded the paper. 'It is my duty as the governor of His Majesty's Prison Solent to inform you that the conviction you received for the murder of Nancy Louise Sayer on 23 November last year has been found to be just and true. Subsequently the sentence of death received on 24 November of the same year has also been upheld. It is therefore also my duty to inform you that the schedule for this sentence to be carried out on 26 October shall be met. All appeals for clemency have been unsuccessful and the sentence shall stand as instructed. Do you understand, Tim?'

'You're saying you never got a call?'

'That's right.'

'I understand.'

The governor reached down and gently clasped his upper arm. 'It's time to go.'

Johnson whispered constantly to Hughes as he attached the waist strap and fitted his arms into the cuffs. Hughes listened intently, as if he was receiving final instructions for his own performance.

The governor led the way out. Riley fell into step with Johnson.

'How are you, Riley?'

He felt the hangman's hand on his back guiding him along the corridor. Riley nodded at the prisoner ahead of them. 'If he can make it, so can I.'

Riley counted his strides. Fourteen led them to the execution chamber. It had changed dramatically since he had been there for practice. Blue drapes covered the walls and blocked the view beneath the gallows. The lighting had been subdued, but he could make out the outlines of people sitting in the gloom along the far wall. This surprised him. He hadn't known there was going to be an audience. He wondered who the fuck they were. Prison officials, government officials, journalists. Probably the lot.

Once inside, the guards disappeared into the background, leaving the governor in front and Riley and Johnson flanking Hughes. The governor steered them to a microphone on a stand by the steps leading up to the gallows. He turned his attention to Hughes.

'Do you want to say anything, Tim?'

Tim Hughes nodded yes and the governor stepped aside. His voice echoed throughout the steel room despite the drapes, like a call from an alpine mountain reaching the valley.

'I would just like it to be recorded that my last thoughts are with my wife, Sylvia, whom I love deeply and never intended to hurt.'

A pause and then a slight movement as if he was readying himself to continue, but instead he retreated from the microphone, head bowed.

As practised, Riley climbed the stairs first, with Hughes behind him and Johnson following them both. The white cotton hood lay on a wooden stool next to the trap-door lever. By the time Riley had lifted the hood, Hughes was already in position, with Johnson once again talking to him constantly in a quiet measured tone. Riley caught the odd phrase. 'That's right. Just relax. Back half a step.' Riley waited to the side of Hughes, while Johnson buckled the leg strap from behind. One thing at a time, the executioner had told him. Otherwise the prisoner will feel surrounded, closed in, and might panic. Johnson stood and nodded. Riley took a step in front of Hughes and raised the hood to put it over his head. Hughes managed a strained smile.

'Goodbye, Riley. Look out for me in the next world.'

'Goodbye, Tim.'

Riley lowered the hood.

Johnson fitted the noose. Riley moved swiftly to the lever and removed the pin. Johnson made a slight adjustment to the noose, a step back, he nodded, Riley pushed and Tim Hughes was gone. The boards beneath Riley shuddered and the body dropped from sight. He heard a noise like a stick being broken over someone's knee and the room took an inward gasp as everyone sucked in air at the same time. The next sound he heard was puking, but he couldn't see the offender in the darkness.

Johnson wrapped an arm around his shoulder. 'OK?'

'Yeah.' His own sense of calm came as a surprise. 'What now? Do we just leave?'

'We have to wait for the doctor to pronounce Hughes dead.'

'I thought he died instantly.'

'Oh, he does.' Johnson squeezed Riley's shoulder reassuringly. 'He did. His heart keeps beating for a time. It's just a physical thing. Like a chicken that keeps on running round a yard despite having its head chopped off.'

'He's a man, not a fucking chicken, Johnson.'

'I know, I know, but it's the same principle.'

'How long will his heart carry on?'

Johnson shrugged. 'Ten to fifteen minutes. Maybe twenty at the most.'

'Twenty fucking minutes.' Riley could feel himself becoming agitated. 'And he doesn't feel a thing?'

'No. Not a thing.' Johnson tried to repeat his squeeze on Riley's shoulder, but Riley slid away from his grip. 'There's no brain activity, Riley. His spinal column is snapped. It's physically impossible for him to feel anything.'

'I don't believe you.' Riley edged to the trap door and peered through the square-cut hole. The curtained-off area of the gallows was illuminated by spotlights. A doctor with stethoscope in hand stood beside the suspended body, accompanied by the guard Simon. As Riley looked on, the doctor stood on a stool, fitted the stethoscope to his ears and listened to the chest of Hughes. Moments later he jumped off the stool and said a few words to Simon, who giggled. As the guard laughed, the body spasmed. The shoulders lifting high into the air. Torso twisting. Legs struggling to bend, to rise, to make it back to solid ground.

Johnson pulled Riley away. 'It's just a physical thing, Riley. He's gone.'

But Riley didn't believe him. Just as when he'd seen the photographs of Nancy and recognized her staring out at him, trapped in the pain and suffering of the moment, he knew that if he was to take the hood off Tim Hughes the man would still be there to ask him why he did it.

The rest of his time in the execution chamber passed in a series of static scenes. Standing on the periphery of a group of men in suits who were all deep in conversation. A guard offering him a stick of chewing gum. A sliver of silver foil he must have missed when unwrapping it clashing badly with one of his fillings. The governor eventually reading a statement into the microphone that Hughes was officially dead.

The canteen stank of fried food. The bacon on his plate sat in a lake of yellow fat and his egg shone with a watery uncooked film. He drank two mugs of coffee and left the breakfast untouched. Every table was busy with the people who had witnessed the execution.

Opposite him Johnson nursed a glass of water.

'Who are all these people, Johnson?'

'I've no idea. Why don't you ask some of them?'

Riley nudged the man next to him, who turned and smiled pleasantly. 'Yes?'

'Who are you? Why are you here?'

'My name is Mathew Van Eldt. I am representing the Dutch government. We are here to see how the death penalty is working in Great Britain. It is interesting that a country such

176

as yours has taken such drastic steps to deal with crime. It is something we have to consider.'

'Holland might bring in the death penalty?'

'It cannot be ruled out. It is here now, why not Holland?'

'And what did you think of the execution?'

'I thought it was carried out very smoothly and efficiently. I was very impressed with the Addison Corporation. You were the man on the platform, weren't you?'

'Yes, I was.' The stink of the food overwhelmed him, his stomach flipped. 'I'm sorry, I have to leave now.' He looked at Johnson and his glass of water. 'I need to get out of here.'

Johnson got to his feet. 'There's a ferry for the mainland in a couple of minutes. I'll take you down to your car.'

Once inside the elevator, Johnson pressed for the appropriate floor and the doors closed. He leaned against the wall and scratched at his left ear. 'So you heard what Mr Van Eldt had to say, but what do you think of the death penalty, Riley?'

'I think it's murder.'

'Of course it is. It's legal murder.' He checked his watch. 'After 6. I better phone home. The wife will be worried.'

'Worried about what?'

'Nothing in particular, she just likes to know that I'm OK. And you, you can return to your normal life now, your wife, girlfriend, kids, whatever you have.'

'I suppose I can, but I don't know how normal it will be.'

'You'll forget, in time.'

'I'm going to try not to. What about you? Do you just wait for another execution, another candidate?'

'That's right, another 18th Pale Descendant.'

The elevator came to rest and the doors opened. Both walked out on to the car deck.

'Why are we called 18th Pale Descendants?'

'As far as I'm aware it's from a poem. "I was shocked and ashamed to discover that I'm the 18th Pale Descendant of some old queen or other." I guess it's a joke. In times gone by it was the monarch who gave the thumbs-down on the criminal to end his life. Now it's all of us. Dig a little and there's a ruthless, heartless soul masquerading itself as justice in every single citizen.'

Johnson waited as Riley unlocked his car.

'Goodbye then, Riley, will you shake my hand?'

Riley reached out for the short stubby fingers. 'Why not? Mine's are as dirty as yours.'

The radio burst into life. 'And at 8.05 the day's headlines once again. Convicted murderer Tim Hughes had his death sentence carried out in the early hours of this morning. Prison authorities issued a statement confirming that Hughes was pronounced dead at 5.28 a.m. The schoolteacher was arrested and found guilty of the killing of his former pupil Nancy Sayer last September.

'MP for Hereford Shirley Conrad still refused to comment on newspaper allegations that she was a regular customer of an escort agency when in the capital. However, she may have more to say after she faces the Prime Minister in a private meeting this afternoon. The meeting comes amid fresh stories in today's papers that she made extensive use of the escort's "extra" services.

'And finally fresh fighting broke out in Chechnya yesterday as Russian forces faced stern resistance in their bid to retake the capital, Grozny. Russian military authorities refused to comment on rebel claims of heavy losses but counter-claimed that the capital will be under their control by nightfall.

'I'm Simon Armitage and you're listening to UK Sounds on 98.5 FM. At 8.07 it's time for the weather and traffic reports with Susie Huxtable.'

Riley already knew the weather. He could see the bright sunshine outside his car window and feel the cold by touching the glass with his hands. He sat parked about twenty yards from his old house. It stood further up the steep hill that was Manor Park Road. There were no other cars on the street. If he eased his handbrake off he would simply roll all the way down to Annandale Street and probably grind to a halt on someone's front lawn.

He got out of the car and strode past the house, taking in great gulps of freezing air. Considering he had hardly slept, he felt remarkably alive. The upstairs curtains were still drawn. Emma, unlike a lot of kids, had never been an early riser. He and Anne had often revelled in laying in late on weekends.

He reached the top of the hill and crossed to where the houses gave way to Manor Park. He followed the grassy slope downwards through a spray of stark bare trees. Dew soaked his shoes and the silver bark of the trees ran with streams of water. The slope levelled out at a concrete path beyond which was a playpark he used to take Emma to.

A figure wandered along the path towards him. An old man wrapped in a full array of winter clothing. Overcoat, hat, scarf and gloves. He dragged a mournful-looking black and white collie behind him. Riley gave him a half-smile of acknowledgement as he passed, which was returned with a raised eyebrow and a hint of suspicion behind square black-rimmed spectacles.

A few yards further on the old man halted to let his dog do what dogs do. Riley grimaced as the dog dropped a series of steaming turds on to the concrete. A few quick steps and Riley had caught up with him.

'Excuse me.'

'What?' the old man replied in a gruff tone.

'What are you doing letting your dog shit all over the path? People use this park. Kids play around here.'

'I'm, eh . . .'

'You're what? Stupid? My daughter plays in this park. I hope you're going to clear this up.'

'I am, yeah, I'll get rid of it.' The old man moved off at pace, tugging the reluctant collie.

Riley stood and watched until he had reached the road at the far side. He laughed at himself. The good citizen. The 18th Pale Descendant.

He hopped on to the roundabout in the playpark and, with a shove of his foot, sent himself spinning slowly in a circle. The tarmac had been replaced by some spongy green safety stuff, but it was still the two slides, a few swings, the seesaw with elephants on each side to sit on and the wooden roundabout with yellow metal bars to hold on to.

Did Emma still like roundabouts? She was only seven, she was bound to still like them. Either that or she had turned into a video junkie without his knowledge. He remembered his dream of her sitting on the swings. Flashing in and out of his sight. It was something he ought to know. It was something he intended to find out.